THE SOUL'S GYMNASIUM

And Other Stories

by

Harold Acton

HAMISH HAMILTON LONDON

First published in Great Britain 1982
by Hamish Hamilton Ltd.
Garden House 57-59 Long Acre London WC2E 9JZ

Copyright   c   1982 by Sir Harold Acton

Acton, Sir Harold
  The soul's gymnasium and other stories.
  I. Title
  823'.912[F]   PR6001.C7

ISBN 0-241-10740-7

Printed in Great Britain by St. Edmundsbury Press
Bury St. Edmunds, Suffolk

CONTENTS

Prologue

'It comes over me even as I write that the general air in which most of these particular flowers of fancy bloom is an air we have pretty well ceased to breathe.'

Henry James: Preface to *Lady Barbarina and Other Tales*, 1922.

Perhaps the gentle reader should have some acquaintance with Florence to savour the essence of these stories.

During the first decade of this century, Florence had a large colony of international expatriates which two world wars, a xenophobic interlude, post-war restrictions and recessions have slowly but surely reduced to a fraction of its former strength. Many of the historic villas owned by foreigners have been sold to speculators who have transformed them into modern apartments, clinics, and hotels, while several have been leased or bequeathed to transatlantic universities. No doubt this was inevitable.

Already in 1877, Henry James observed that 'if one is a stranger half the talk is about villas . . . Their extraordinary largeness and massiveness are a satire upon their present fate. They were not built with such a thickness of wall and depth of embrasure, such a solidity of staircase and superfluity of stone, simply to afford an economical winter residence to English and American families.' At that time, he wrote, 'most of them are offered to rent (many of them for sale) at prices unnaturally low: you may have a tower and a garden, a chapel and an expanse of thirty windows, for five hundred dollars a year.'

Many Anglo-American families were to settle permanently in these country houses, extensions of ancient farms and pleasure grounds. In most cases their occupation was beneficial: the buildings were restored and furnished with taste, the gardens were carefully cultivated (though some were fashionably Anglicized, not always an improvement). A few, like the Villa Palmieri at San Domenico and the Villa Medici at Fiesole had had English residents since the eighteenth century.

Apart from the light cost of living the valley of Arno enjoyed a salubrious reputation. The fragile Elizabeth Barrett Browning felt 'the climate so divine and the way of doing things so serene and suited to our tastes and instincts' that she recovered enough strength to climb the hill of Bellosguardo on foot. But in those days the city walls had not been demolished and they must have modified the *tramontana*, the fierce north wind, for Florence was favoured as a winter resort, especially by retired Anglo-Indian officers and civil servants. Yet it can be the hottest of Italian cities and the coldest.

Above all, it was the unique cultural atmosphere, the persistent aura of supreme poets and artists, which gave foreigners a soothing sense of uplift, even of superiority. Their daily lives might be humdrum but they were surrounded by beauty, they were saturated with it even subconsciously. The most articulate section were the writers, painters, art historians and collectors who found perennial inspiration in the city and its population past and present, perhaps more past than present.

Some of the English became more emphatically English through living abroad, some Americans more American: they imported their native customs and cooking and led the same sort of existence as in Surrey or Massachusetts. Excellent servants were available who often managed the house for their employers and regarded themselves as part of the family in a truly democratic spirit. Inwardly some regarded themselves as more civilized than these outsiders who made such a fuss about comparative trivialities. Daily hip baths forsooth, and all those cups of tea! Five-meals-a-day folk, and what heavy meals!

Discussing the oddities of this evaporating species, how often have I been asked: 'Why don't you write about them? They would make an amusing novel.' But the novel seemed too prolix a medium, and short stories seemed more appropriate. Few of my protagonists were sufficiently interesting in themselves; none were heroes or heroines involved in social or political movements; none were underdogs or underbitches belonging to a 'submerged population group', as recommended material for short stories by Mr Frank O'Connor. Yet their individual flavour was undeniable, stuffed (as Norman Douglas would say) with whimsicality and abstractions.

Till the outbreak of the 1914-18 war the society they salted and peppered might aptly be described as *fin-de-siècle*. Each a centre of his special little world, they were still living placidly in the eighteen-nineties, of which the two Reginalds, Turner and Temple, were prominent survivors.

Reggie Turner prolonged the style, the mannerisms, the persiflage of the Yellow Book period, and the voice of Oscar Wilde could be heard, as at a séance, when he recounted his exploits. In his reflective essay on 'Laughter' Max Beerbohm portrayed Reggie as *Comus*, his mobile features 'somewhat akin to the comic mask of the ancients', his mellifluous intonation, versatile mimicry, and spontaneous repartee. Having produced a round dozen of anodyne novels he concentrated his genius on friendship and conversation. What a conjuror of improbable fantasies when he was in the mood, preferably before an impromptu audience! What a fine comedian was lost by his innate modesty! Unfortunately his wit failed to permeate his writings, though his judgement of books was perceptive and he was the first person I heard to pay tribute to Marcel Proust. In this he might have been influenced by C. K. Scott Moncrieff who was translating *A la recherche du temps perdu* in Florence at the time — fifty pages a day, I was told.

The rival Reggie, Temple, had hoped to become an actor, but he was frustrated by his small physique. The stage was his secret passion and Eleonora Duse was his divinity. Impeccably neat, pink and fair, he looked a dandy beside Reggie Turner, and his surface was more conventional. I nicknamed him Earl

Lavender for there was usually a touch of mauve about his shirts and handkerchiefs. His alternative for a stage career was to paint exact replicas of early Tuscan predellas, so precise that even cracks and wormholes were included. By these and the decoration of little boxes in eighteenth-century style, which he varnished and revarnished until they resembled genuine *vernis Martin*, he added to his modest income. He had an unexpected penchant for the macabre and told horrifying stories in a quiet voice, yet he shunned the Bohemian weirdies and what is now called 'camp'. His code of manners was distinctly late Victorian. He winced at the other Reggie and he heartily disapproved of Robert de la Condamine.

Extremely flamboyant and paradoxical, Condamine appeared occasionally on the London stage under the name of Farquharson when, in the rôle of Herod or the mad Czar Paul of Russia, his exaggerated stammer vanished. In a drawing-room his stammer was embarrassingly effective: it emphasized his ninetyish epigrams. It was hard to control one's laughter. Was he as young as he looked or as old as rumour alleged? He might have been any age between thirty and sixty with or without the aid of cosmetics. The reality beneath his mask remained ambiguous. His green volume 'The Upper Garden' provides no clue, for it reads like Marius the Epicurean bemused by marijuana.

Among the writers such temporary residents as D.H. Lawrence, Aldous Huxley and Norman Douglas have left copious records, and Lawrence has caricatured a characteristic group of cronies in 'Aaron's Rod'. Ronald Firbank was caviare to the general. A solitary disjointed figure, neurotically shy, he writhed in contemplation of the peaches he pecked at in Betti's restaurant; on the Via Tornabuoni his capering walk with an enormous bunch of lilies would have been conspicuous even in a crowd of beatniks, like an exotic biped strayed from a menagerie.

Gordon Craig and Isadora Duncan were fascinating even from a distance. I regretted I was too young to know them personally, but I admired Gordon Craig's woodcuts in *The Mask* and was dazzled by the rhythmic grace of Isadora. In the streets then blessedly free from motor traffic Isadora had the pavement to herself, a Grecian goddess moving to stately inner music. In her autobiography she wrote of Gordon Craig's constant state of exaltation: 'an ordinary walk through the streets with him was like a promenade in Thebes of ancient Egypt with a superior High Priest.' It was an exaltation which she shared in Florence, where she danced at the Arena Goldoni.

The literary bluestockings — Vernon Lee at Maiano and Janet Ross at Poggio Gherardo — had a wider range of interests than those we meet today, and a deeper knowledge of Italy. They had hobnobbed with J. A. Symonds and Henry James. Radclyffe Hall flaunted her feminism in masculine attire, but she was no intellectual and Florence made little impact on her parish-pump provincialism.

Yielding to the persuasion of younger friends, I have tried to evoke the atmosphere of this vanished society in the short fictions gathered into this volume. None of the characters are directly drawn from life but several are based on former residents of Florence. One or two are composite portraits, the Marchesa Carrie and Leo of the Ivory Tower for instance, but in both these tales I have allowed my fancy to embroider freely on the subject. The Marchesa's language was sometimes too crude for polite readers to swallow and in that respect she belonged to the avant-garde, or to a previous century. One recalls the anecdote of Sarah, Duchess of Marlborough, calling on Lord Mansfield. When told that he was not at home she refused to leave her name. His lordship's secretary, in describing the unknown visitor, said: 'I could not make out who she was, but she swore so dreadfully that she must be a lady of quality.' Of 'Marchesa Carrie' Sir Max Beerbohm wrote: * 'I felt as I sat listening to my hostess's conversation, that I was having a beautiful dinner in a cesspool.'

* *Max Beerbohm: Letters to Reggie Turner, London 1964, p. 245*

The model for Leo of the Ivory Tower was a distinguished art collector, but this is another composite portrait or *collage*. Florence used to pullulate with foreign art collectors, most of whom, obsessed with their eternal treasure hunt, became detached from ordinary life. Theirs was a consuming hunger for the painting or sculpture or cassone which had caught their fancy and set it ablaze. Not a few, like Herbert Horne, would sacrifice their bodily comforts, their families and friends, to the acquisition of an object beyond their financial means. Some had to sell in order to buy, with much anguish and haggling and heart-burning. They were wholly possessed by their possessions, inanimate to others but human to themselves. This made them seem cranky to less acquisitive mortals. An Italian dealer-collector of my acquaintance, a person of exquisite taste and uncommon flair, was so shabby and unkempt that he might have been mistaken for a beggar. He burst into tears when he was tempted by a rich purchaser to part with one of his rarities. 'I paid for it with my blood,' he sobbed, in an apartment cluttered with other priceless objects, all of which had their price.

Sir Osbert Sitwell has stippled a broader panorama of bygone Florentine society in his magnificent memoirs, which are dominated by the personality of his father Sir George, another compulsive art collector. 'On the Continent' (1957), the third volume of Sir Osbert's poems, 'England Reclaimed', dealt more particularly with English residents and visitors abroad, and though he stated that the persons described 'have not existed physically, only in the realm of imagination', several are recognisable cartoons of Anglo-Florentines I knew: his Milordo Inglese Lord Henry Somerset; Algernon Braithwaite Reggie Turner; Algernon Petre Reggie Temple; Donald McDougall Norman Douglas; Gino of the Bookshop Pino Orioli.

In my stories I have not poached on this preserve. What my characters have in common is the all-embracing Tuscan background. They pursued their avocations in a more leisurely, and perhaps a more carefree, age than that through which we are gravitating, before the multiplication of television sets, electronics, and the threat of a nuclear Armageddon. Even in the last quarter of a century the conditions in which some survived have ceased to obtain, which may give these tales the patina of ancient history.

Now hostesses are generally associated with aeroplanes. As for the private art collector, he has been figuratively castrated by the mass museum curator with gargantuan Getty funds at his disposal. The curator is obliged to be eclectic. His taste is subordinate to expertise, which is quite a different matter. Hitherto we have benefited from the flair of the private collector, who followed his own star (often invisible to his contemporaries) through thick and thin. Moralists have blamed him for valuing property more than people. Certainly he is a fish out of water in a socialist world.

The type of collector in 'A Phantom Botticelli' and in 'Leo's Ivory Tower' is all but extinct. The private collections it was my privilege to visit in Florentine palaces and villas when I was young are either dispersed like Charles Loeser's, or bequeathed to the city like Herbert Horne's, or to a university like Berenson's.

Martin Wilmer in 'A Phantom Botticelli' is purely fictitious, though personal incidents have crept into the narrative. I suffered from a similar burglary since permitting large groups of art-lovers to visit my father's collection of Tuscan Primitives. The latter had hung undisturbed for half a century or more.

In spite of Henry James's contention that the collecting spirit is 'the most modern of our current passions', it has always existed. There are the squirrel collectors who hoard their treasures like nuts and keep them locked in cabinets for furtive communion, and the proud extroverts who enjoy exhibiting them. However, Henry James understood the anguish of a dedicated connoisseur whose children fail to care for the beautiful objects he spent his happiest years assembling. Since

'The Spoils of Poynton', death duties and punitive taxation have caused the dispersal of many great art collections. Fortunately the National Trust has helped to preserve a majority in England, but there is nothing of the kind in Italy.

With all due respect and veneration for Henry James, it is high time that his laboured thesis of American innocence versus European corruption was exploded. I have witnessed too much evidence of the contrary, naïve young Italians jilted by American minxes or seduced by the promise of a trip to Eldorado. Many a simple southerner is bewildered by those rapid coitions of sympathy followed by indifference and oblivion. The lure of a rich girl from Buffalo trying to discover her identity at the cost of poor Europeans is well illustrated in Mabel Dodge Luhan's 'European Experiences' (1935) from which I derived the kernel of 'Fin de Race'. Candid, light-hearted, all out for fun and new sensations, the type fails to realize when she is playing with fire. This is due to lack of imagination rather than to wantonness, but the result is equally deplorable. 'Flora's Lame Duck' needs no further commentary: it is a satire on the best of intentions.

In 'Codicil Coda' the scene was transferred to London, though its heroine was the seasonal chatelaine of a luxurious Florentine villa. Here truth was stranger than the fiction with which it is blended, for Muriel played the *grande dame* of royal descent in a perpetual charade of her own improvisation. Every knick-knack in her drawing-room was allotted a picturesque pedigree: a flexible silver salmon had been presented by Peter the Great to one of her ancestors; a smaller fish of enamelled metal was attributed to Benvenuto Cellini, while duplicates of both could be found on the Ponte Vecchio.

Her guests were commanded to curtsey or bow to dubious connections of the Bourbons and Bonapartes. Retired consuls were introduced as ambassadors. Everything was magnified by her delusion of grandeur. If, as often happened, thirteen were invited to dinner by oversight — some serene highness had turned up on the spur of the moment — the thirteenth was peremptorily dismissed with a flea in his ear. And at dinner a liver pâté bought from a neighbouring grocer was said to have been flown in from Strasbourg for the occasion. Titles meant more to her than their owners. Often the latter were dowdy duchesses and penurious dukes, a dim *von* or a *zu*, only too delighted to be piloted through the old palaces with pomp and ceremony. It was prescriptive to keep her hosts waiting for the arrival of her distinguished suite while everybody was dying for a drink. One of the last professional Edwardians, her caprices were topics of general hilarity. I hope I have not been unfair to dear old Muriel, for she had a strain of poetic fantasy which is becoming rare. There are even moments when I miss her.

'Saint Gabriel' provides a more spiritual example of mythomania — the sanctification of a frivolous husband. By contrast Hector Neal in 'The Soul's Gymnasium' is a sybaritical seeker after strange gods who took to theosophy, astrology, and psychotherapy in later life. What started as a mere hobby became a ruling obsession. ('Obsessions' occurred to me as a sub-title for these stories but it sounded too Freudian.)

'A morning at Upshott's' transfers the patient reader to London, for I have yet to discover a comparable bookshop in Florence since Pino Orioli left us. Upshott's is partly a projection of wishful thinking. Among the A's on a shelf, or climbing over each other in piles on the floor, that is where my own publications can be found, even those long forgotten and out of print.

Subconsciously it might have been suggested by a French eighteenth-century engraving of a bookseller's stall opposite a haberdasher's in a Parisian arcade, *La Galerie du Palais*. The bookseller is extolling his latest editions to a couple of swells, whose attention is distracted by the charm of a young lady at the opposite counter. One of them remarks to the bookseller: 'That face is worth more than all your songs!'

Having left the amorous couple at Upshott's, we return to a

nest of singing birds in Florence. How a mediocre poet is launched to ephemeral fame by a doting wife is the theme of 'The Narcissus Elegy'. Having convinced herself that her handsome husband is a genius, Chloe could well afford to convince others with abundant creature comforts as a bait. Adrian's frail Muse is fed artificially, and when Chloe dies his Muse dies with her. He turns to philosophy, grows a long beard, and emigrates to Patmos. Sad, very sad, but at least Chloe died with her illusions intact.

Often the story I planned has assumed a different form in the process of composition, and I confess that these are very unlike the stories I had in mind. Perhaps I should have woven them into a picaresque novel. Alas, it is too late. May the reader forgive me for not telling him about 'a submerged population group', though time has submerged most of my characters.

The Marchesa Carrie

'I don't want my clocks to be wound up any longer, Attilio. I'm tired of their ticking and striking. For goodness sake let them stop.'

'But the clock-winder is waiting downstairs. He will be heartbroken. He is a poor man with a family, Signora, and your patronage is precious to him.'

'Then tell him to come all the same. He may dust them or oil them or polish them, so long as they don't go on ticking.'

'How shall we know what the time is? Nobody in the house will be punctual.'

'The kitchen clock must suffice — so long as I don't hear it. The church-bells are good enough for me.'

And indeed the bells of Florence were very dear to Carrie. She had loved them since her first visit as a schoolgirl, and could distinguish between their chimes at all hours. Whereas clocks were merciless: they made her feel *passée* every mortal minute. *Basta*! she scolded them. *Silenzio*!

Albeit long past the age of amorous dalliance — she was nearer eighty than seventy — Carrie was prone to talk of little else. Invariably the conversation in her spacious salon drifted towards the perennial topic of who was engaged to whom and, preferably, who was having an affair with whom. The callow young concerned her less than the mature in whose category she fancied herself to belong: far more engrossing were the adventures of those who could look back on years of extra-marital escapades. Ripeness was all but domesticity was dull. Yet Carrie had been faithful to three husbands, each older than herself.

Early in life she discovered that bawdy talk could be an

1

effective substitute for physical attraction. Rabelaisian ribaldry from the lips of gentility could be irresistibly comic, and Carrie, though you would not guess it, was descended from a respectable Virginian family ruined by the civil war. In her scurrilous vein she had no Florentine competitors. She kept an album of limericks in her boudoir for which she solicited contributions from literary celebrities, but after a glance at its contents they recoiled with crimson faces. The few who regarded it as an invitation to misbehave were soon shown the difference between words and deeds.

Carrie was already a widow of indeterminate age when Benjamin Royston proposed to her. A retired English stockbroker with a cockney accent, Ben cherished an ambition to make a splash in Florentine society. By himself he was too uncouth to appeal to what he termed 'the posh upper crust.' He had been standing drinks at the club for donkey's years but his generosity had not been reciprocated by fellow members. The same types loitered round the bar for free potations until Ben concluded that this was not leading him anywhere near his goal. He needed an enterprising hostess and Carrie possessed the vital qualifications. His divorced wife had been pretty but unsatisfactory — so unsatisfactory that he had grown indifferent to feminine pulchritude. Carrie could be described as *piquante*, and her trim figure, immaculately garbed, helped to compensate for her lack of facial symmetry. It was one of her naughty stories, or perhaps her limerick about the 'young plumber of Leigh who was plumbing a girl by the sea', which encouraged him to propose to her. He had been shy of her sophisticated manner until then. The story or the limerick — he had forgotten which after a double whisky — had served to break the ice. Though his plumbing days were over it had been a truly companionate marriage. Together they turned one of the grandest Cinquecento palaces into a liberty hall for the 'posh upper crust' and Ben revelled in his role as Amphitryon.

Florentines had long been accustomed to eccentric foreigners, and when their eccentricity was counterbalanced with lavish hospitality they were none too finical about the quarterings of their hosts. If Ben were boorish under the influence of booze, Carrie made everybody comfortable. Innumerable tables neatly disposed for card-games as well as for chess, mah-jong and dominoes, within reach of a magnificent buffet, were among the principal allurements of the Royston palazzo.

At last Ben could survey 'the cream of the cream' with a proprietary air. He welcomed them all with Pickwickian effusion. Never mind if his memory for names was wobbly and he confused the Contessas with the Marchesas, Carrie would explain who was who and whisper the most important names into his one operative ear. Moreover Attilio, the indispensable majordomo, was a mine of arcane information about the Florentine gentry. He was as conversant with their genealogy as with the state of their finances and in crucial cases he warned Carrie against those he deemed undesirable. 'That little Count Moroni is *poco raccomandabile*,' he informed her. 'He was arrested in a place of public convenience.'

'So what? That's none of your business. I invite whom I please here,' she snapped at him.

Attilio shrugged his shoulders. 'I speak for your benefit, Signora. The scandal is too notorious.'

Though Carrie was vexed she ceased to invite the shady Count to her receptions.

Attilio kept a lynx eye on the card players so that the winners should leave him an adequate gratuity. If they were remiss he would exercise his right of veto: the Signori were not at home, or were otherwise engaged, or had gone abroad for an indefinite period. Habitués soon grasped that they must keep on the right side of Attilio. An open hand was significantly extended when he escorted them to the front door.

A tall figure with aquiline features, wavy hair of an improbable yellow, and a supercilious gait, he looked far more distinguished than the host. Carrie assured her intimates that he was the natural son of a Roman duke, and there was no

3

doubt he felt superior to most of her guests, some of whom he treated with a familiarity verging on insolence. While helping the half-paralysed Major Frisby into his overcoat, for instance, he patted his posterior. And when he knelt to adjust the fallen shoe-buckle of a royal duchess he exclaimed: 'How many a courtier would be jealous of this privilege, your Highness!' Both the duchess and the major were flattered by these attentions but sometimes he went too far. To the gluttonous Baron Lisi piling his plate with an exorbitant bunch of asparagus, he observed: 'Better watch your outline, sir, you are putting on too much paunch.'

Some called Attilio 'the boss', and indeed Carrie was often swayed by his suggestions. She appreciated the special tone he gave to her gatherings: his service was impeccable, his flower arrangements were superb. None could adorn a dinner table with such elegance, and his decoration was always different. 'I wish I could steal Attilio from you,' said more than one envious dowager. But Attilio suited the Royston palazzo and he knew it. No lucrative offer could tempt him from a position so mutually congenial. His only foible was an exaggerated penchant for perfume.

'What is that scent you are using?' Carrie asked him.

'*L'heure exquise*, Madam. May I offer you some?'

'It's too strong. You smell like a tart.'

'A fresh tart among stale ones, Madam. None of your guests have taken a bath this morning. One must defend one's nostrils.'

'Let me present you with some eau-de-Cologne. It is less pungent.'

But she could not wean him from the scent bottle.

For Ben Royston he acted as valet and nurse combined. He selected the shirt, suit, necktie appropriate to every function; he even shaved him and trimmed his shaggy hair. Since marriage to Carrie, Ben's exterior had improved. He had never been so cosseted before, but his temper had not improved with his appearance and he often rebelled against his more predatory guests, whatever their status. When he caught one of them filling his pockets from a box of Havana cigars he flipped the box out of his hand and said gruffly: 'Now you put all those back into the box and take one. And mind you smoke it here and now.' Which did not prevent the brazen fellow from returning to the palazzo for more of the same, though Attilio was told to keep him under observation. Others were apt to cram their cases with his Turkish cigarettes, but this was too usual to deserve notice.

Ben had a tendency to explode when he felt he was being 'put upon'. He was particularly annoyed with guests who retired after dinner when he wanted them for bridge. 'Having gorged and guzzled fit to burst, I suppose you are going to a whoreshop to work it off. You needn't put your nose in my house again,' he told a pompous ex-diplomat.

Purple in the face, with popping bloodshot eyes, it became evident that Ben was heading for apoplexy. Carrie became so embarrassed by his sudden tantrums that when he had his fatal stroke she was inwardly relieved. 'A blessing in disguise,' was the general verdict.

Amply rewarded for enlivening Ben's old age, Carrie had no cause to repine. Old herself, though her age was a well-guarded secret, she was rejuvenated by her widow's weeds. Black tulle suited her, and the black was soon turned to discreet mauve and silvery grey. The pretext of widowhood permitted her to revise her list of guests: Ben's gambling cronies and the topers with questionable titles were expunged. Attilio was a useful counsellor in the weeding process: he paid off many an old score. From a snobbish point of view the quality of Carrie's guests was sublimated.

Ben's funeral was as quiet as it could be. Attilio deputized for Carrie at the cremation and saw that Ben's ashes were deposited in a coffin in order not to offend Catholic sensibilities. A weeping angel of Carrara marble, chosen by Attilio, guarded Ben's tomb in the Allori cemetery.

Carrie took advantage of her period of mourning to have her

face lifted in Paris. A drooping eyelid and a pendulous dewlap had perturbed her to the point of obsession. She was aware that she was no beauty but at least her face could be tidied up. The transformation was amazingly successful. Widowhood seemed to agree with her. She never suffered from loneliness, for though she had ceased to keep open house she continued to entertain on an exclusive scale. The gastronomic fame of her dinners made even a belated invitation desirable, and her repertoire of naughty stories never flagged. 'Carrie says things that *only* she could say,' as the dowager Duchess of Trasimene expressed it. 'Her freedom of speech is a tonic.'

Two exotic priests were the latest recruits to Carrie's inner circle, but after each had said grace in turn the conversation swam in its customary channels. Monsignor Vaya, of noble Hungarian birth, and Father Kourakin, a princely Muscovite with a golden beard, introduced an *obbligato* of picturesque piety into Carrie's pagan salon, frescoed with Leda and the swan, Ganymede with the eagle, and Bacchanalian scenes from classical mythology. Mythology less classical monopolized the meal, with Carrie shedding fresh light on some unsuspected liaison.

Her older friends were puzzled by this ecclesiastical incursion until Monsignor Vaya's announcement that Carrie had been received into the Church. The chapel in the palace having been renovated, guests were invited to midday Mass before Sunday luncheon. Carrie's conversation startled her sceptical intimates. The most mundane of hostesses fingering a rosary blessed by the Pope; lives of the saints interspersed with those scurrilous limericks on her table — surely some mystery lurked behind it. She had become even sprightlier since her conversion. 'Late, but not too late to save my immortal soul,' she said. 'Repentance is delicious and I've fallen in love with my godfather.'

The biggest surprise was held in reserve, for her godfather was identified with that venerable knight of Malta Marchese Luigi degli Amidei, who had been an ascetic widower for half a century. Apart from his advanced age and great wealth he was a pillar of tradition, Tuscan to the backbone, proud of the antiquity of his lineage. In early boyhood he had been a page to the last Grand Duke of Tuscany. 'We were better off then than now,' he said, 'and taxes were infinitesimal.' But he hitched his wagon to the rising star of Mussolini, who had presented him with a signed photograph. What had he in common with Carrie? Only Attilio knew.

Since Ben Royston's demise the Marchese had been Carrie's daily visitor at hours when nobody else was admitted to her apartments, of which he was the landlord. They played bezique together every evening or merely sat in confabulation holding hands like two young lovers, and Carrie accompanied him to his country estates near Siena and in the Maremma. Gradually they became inseparable. The Marchese was captivated by her flights of fancy alternating with practical advice, and Carrie was enchanted by his chivalrous assiduity.

As none of her acquaintances had an inkling of this friendship they were stunned by the news of her marriage. Carrie of the *risqué* anecdote and shocking limerick, the vivacious widow of a gross vulgarian, now an authentic Marchesa with armorial bearings of millennial antiquity! — yet she had not changed her style for all that. Translated into her Anglo-American Italian, her stories were even funnier than in English, and the old Marchese was reduced to helpless laughter by her rendition of 'the plumber of Leigh'. When he had to send for the *trombaio* Attilio was perplexed by the Marchese's merriment. Not all the limericks in Carrie's album were worthy of translation and some had to be expurgated. Her fantasy ran riot when she described the rapture of confession. 'I love to tease my confessor. But I suspect the Monsignor is getting deaf, for he always assures me that my sins are venial.' And indeed her private life had been blameless. She had never deceived a husband, and she would have flinched from the physical reality of seduction. Her boastful accounts of nuptial nights were pure, or impure, fiction. It was

7

impossible to visualize the octogenarian Marchese as a Casanova. But as he walked arm in arm with her, or gazed tenderly into her eyes, it was clear that he doted on Carrie. He chuckled at her jokes like a schoolboy, but unlike her previous mates he was abstemious. Let others carouse: he enjoyed their enjoyment as part of a comedy.

Frugal in her own diet, (yoghurt and a boiled egg), Carrie took pride in the aesthetic triumphs of her chef, nicknamed Escoffier though he came from the Abruzzi. At the sight of his Gothic castles of ice-cream and spun sugar the guests clapped their hands and cheered. Unfortunately the polyglot conversation was inferior in quality to his elaborate creations. With such sumptuous fare it was difficult for the mind to soar towards higher things. Eyes wandered towards the salmon and the *coquelet en pâte*; mouths twitched and fingers itched for a second helping, while Carrie tried to inveigle the company into indiscretions. Even the priests were distracted by the dishes. Without understanding the gist of Carrie's badinage they radiated benevolence. 'Poor ducks, they have only one meal a day,' she explained. 'It's good for them to come out into the world. Monsignor Vaya has a cell in a monastery, you know, freezing in winter and tropical in summer, but I've never heard him complain. He's an absolute saint. So is Father Kourakin. I don't know which is the saintlier but both deserve haloes. Father Kourakin was a great landowner before the Russian revolution. All his family were raped before they were buried alive and he was saved by a fluke. We must get him to tell us about it. I often go to the Russian church on Viale Milton just for the music. He can sing like Chaliapin, it's very uplifting.'

The only skeletons at the feast were two of the Marchese's nephews, who resented his marriage not only as a misalliance but as a serious threat to their patrimony. What could the old man see in this grotesque and frivolous outsider? The extravagance of his new mode of life alarmed them: the endless banquets, the large retinue of livered retainers, a new Isotta

8

Fraschini instead of the vintage Fiat, trips to Bad Gastein instead of to Montecatini, yelping greyhounds and screeching parrots . . . And the *Befana*, as they dubbed her, was encrusted with their family jewels. One comfort was that it could not last. Their Uncle Luigi's life-expectancy was limited and the *Befana* might wear him out.

In their moth-eaten tail-coats redolent of camphor the elderly twins were ushered up the grand staircase of their ancestral palace and announced by Attilio at the door of the salon ablaze with chandeliers to kiss the outstretched hand of Zia Carrie beside Zio Luigi, whose chest glowed with the stars and ribands of various Orders. It was like a scene in an opera, a glaring contrast with their bucolic existence in the Maremma.

Attilio sniffed and winked at the Marchesa, who was amused by their candid bewilderment. 'You smell of moth-balls,' she remarked. 'Let me spray you with *Quelques fleurs*!'

'We never dress for dinner in the Maremma,' they explained apologetically. 'We live like Horace on his Sabine farm.'

'That must be wholesome but dull. Where are your wives? I hoped you would bring them along.'

'With so many grandchildren to look after they had to stay at home. They seldom venture out at night.'

'We must find them an English nanny. I'll make enquiries immediately. Country life would not suit me — far too cramping. I hope you have nice neighbours. What on earth do you find to do?'

'We are busy from morning till night. Farming is a full-time occupation.'

'Well, I'm glad you could join us this evening. Perhaps it's a relief to get away from your wives.'

'I never want to leave my Carrie,' said the Marchese sententiously. After a six-course dinner there was dancing in the ball-room to the strains of Rajola's band. When they played the *Blue Danube* Carrie seized Luigi's arm and away they whirled together, round and round. The nephews goggled at the spectacle: their uncle must be tougher than they

9

imagined. Carrie told them she was taking him to Lausanne for a hormone cure, after which they would go to St Moritz for golf at Samaden. Hans Badrutt had promised them the royal suite at the Palace Hotel. Half the Roman aristocracy would be there — she rattled through a catalogue of princely names — so it ought to be festive. The nephews tried to look interested as she prattled on about her plans for the summer but, unaccustomed to such late hours and so rich a repast, they smothered yawn after yawn.

'Poor boys, you should go to bye-byes.' said Carrie, 'you look fairly pooped. What about some more bubbly? This is Dom Perignon, but there's Mumm if you prefer it.'

'Veuve Cliquot, Signora Marchesa,' Attilio corrected her.

'Strega would be more appropriate.' But the *double entendre* passed over Carrie's head.

'There's no accounting for tastes. Give them Strega, Attilio.'

'I regret we have none in the house. We have Courvoisier, Armagnac, Grand Marnier . . .'

They chose mineral water and said 'Chin-chin' as they sipped it. From their point of view the evening had not been agreeable. While they congratulated their uncle on his youthful vivacity their hearts sank at the thought of all the money he was spending: though Carrie was reputed to be affluent they felt sure that Luigi would have to foot the bill. The band was still playing when they bowed their way back to their battered motor. Attilio did not deign to hint for a tip. A few bridge-players lingered on as if hypnotized by their cards. Some people never knew when to go home. Carrie left them to their game.

Summer in St Moritz was like a prolonged fashion show whose protagonists changed their costume several times a day, with the Darby and Joan from Florence in the foreground, whether on the golf links or on the dance floor. The hormone treatment in Lausanne had paid visible dividends and the air of the Engadine intensified their energy. They were known to their arthritic coevals as 'the Indomitables.'

They were setting forth to picnic on a glacier when a telegram arrived for Luigi. 'I have such a dread of telegrams,' said Carrie. 'Please don't open it, not till this evening. I'm sure it can bear to wait.'

But it was marked urgent and Luigi could not resist. His hands trembled and his face became clouded. Bad news, of course. Both the Maremma twins, as Carrie called his nephews, had been killed in a motor accident. A tyre of their old Fiat had burst and they had been flung against a wall which had fractured their skulls. Though Carrie attempted to dissuade him Luigi insisted on returning for the funeral. Let us be thankful that we are alive, she thought, we are living on borrowed time. Let the dead bury their dead. Luigi's funeral and hers could not be far enough distant. The nephews had plenty of children and a brother in the Argentine, so the family would not die out. That should console the patriarch in Luigi. She wondered guiltily about her strange lack of emotion. For herself she had no horror of death and if, as she dimly believed, there was a next world, she had no desire to meet the majority of those she had known in this one, including her previous husbands. Their faces floated before her and she could hear their reproachful voices, filling her with the gloom she had struggled to suppress. Regardless of her Swiss specialist's advice she ordered a double Martini.

In spite of a sedative she slept uneasily that night, for the prospect of returning to Florence out of season to attend a funeral with Luigi's boring relations aggravated her gloom. She hoped Monsignor Vaya would help her to face the ordeal. The service was to be held in the palace chapel, but could it accommodate a whole mob of mourners? How maddening of the nephews to be killed so inopportunely . . . Fortunately Attilio would cope with the family invasion. What a blessing to possess such a butler. Comforted by the sound of Luigi's snoring, Carrie dozed off.

As she had feared, the homeward journey from St Moritz with its change from cool altitude to blazing heat was

11

exhausting. Most of Luigi's relations and dependants, the factors and farmers of his estates, gathered round him with the hackneyed rhetoric of condolence. The widows and their children clung to him and wept copiously throughout the funeral service.

'*Requiem aeternam dona eis, Domine, et lux perpetua luceat eis. . .*' Reluctant tears rolled from Carrie's eyes while Luigi mumbled the words after the priest. But the passage about that dreadful day 'when heaven and earth shall quake and the world be purged by fire' made her feel hypocritical about her conversion. For once she felt as if Luigi were a stranger, that he belonged to a different civilization. After standing beside him to thank all the people who drew up in a queue to kiss her and press her hand, Carrie retreated to her bedroom with a sick headache. She wanted to drag Luigi away with her, but he was besieged by the wives of his nephews bombarding him with questions about their problems. They were too self-concerned to notice his extreme pallor and fatigue. Suddenly he collapsed and had to be carried to the nearest sofa.

It had been a heart attack from which he never recovered. For the third time Carrie found herself a widow. Her premonition had been justified: those wretched nephews had not only killed themselves, they had hastened the death of their uncle. Carrie felt more indignant than disconsolate. Without the practical support of Attilio she too would have collapsed.

The Marchese was laid out in state with all his Orders as a knight of Malta in the Amidei chapel, and again Carrie had to receive the visitors who arrived to condole with her. How she wished she could engage a substitute as, heavily veiled, she shook hands with them all. It will be my turn next, she mused, but I'm not ready yet. I'll keep them waiting.

Attilio had arranged a mammoth buffet for the mourners, of whom Luigino, known as 'the young Marchese' though he was fifty odd, was the most prominent, having flown from the Argentine for the funeral of his brothers. He was now the chief

12

male heir of the Amidei and as such he had never approved of his uncle's 'morganatic marriage'. Rumours of Carrie's prodigality had followed him to Buenos Aires and now he was confronted with the gaudy evidence: all the family plate on display in the dining room, the finest set of Ginori porcelain with the Amidei crest, and enough victuals to feed a regiment of *Bersaglieri*. How greedily the mourners piled their plates! Their gourmandizing destroyed his appetite. Glumly he gazed at the portraits of his ancestors on the walls: even they seemed to frown on this wanton extravagance. Remembering his uncle's frugality in the past, he blamed Carrie.

'Poor Luigino, he looks disconsolate. He must have been really fond of the old man though they never got on when he was alive. He was always kept short of cash and running into debt.'

'Well, now he has inherited most of the property. Six country houses and hundreds of hectares. The Marchesa is to keep the town palace and the villa near Lucca during her lifetime but Luigino will be saddled with the heaviest death duties. Poor Luigino, he's had to wait so long, and now he's over fifty and old for his age. What a picture of misery!'

'Don't expect me to feel sorry for him. He's better off than most of us Florentines. And he'd have been less well off if his brothers had survived. The town palace will soon be his, for the Marchesa can't live for ever. What will he do with it when he gets it? He's only a bachelor . . .'

'A very eligible one. All the girls will run after him.'

'He is said to prefer the boys.'

'*Cela n'empêche pas*. Competition will be keener...'

Carrie bore her bereavement with exemplary fortitude. With what Luigino considered indecent haste — though time was doubly precious at her age — Carrie gave the same luncheons and dinners, at first limited to six for bridge or backgammon, *tenue de ville*; but after a month the number was increased. 'Life is a series of beginnings,' she said, 'and at my age one cannot afford to retire . . . No, I am not considering

13

remarriage as you suppose. In future it will have to be a hot-water bottle instead of a bed-companion.'

Luigino made a point of refusing her invitations for, as he candidly remarked, she should not be encouraged to squander his patrimony. Attilio was encouraging her for all she was worth and Luigino could do nothing but curse him under his breath. What worried him was her sudden interest in art, since various connoisseurs had opened her eyes to the value of the pictures on her walls. Hitherto she had scarcely noticed them, except 'Susanna and the Elders' and 'The Woman taken in Adultery' which provoked her irreverent mirth. Now she had them cleaned and restored with brilliant results. Museum directors applied for permission to see them and have them photographed; they went into ecstasies and even offered to buy them, naming sums that took her breath away. 'I wouldn't dream of parting with any of them,' she said.

'Please think it over. You may take a fancy to something different. You've so many Old Masters here that would be displayed to better advantage in a museum. That "Flight into Egypt" for instance: it's lost among all those Primitives. I hope you will change your mind. If so, I'm at your disposal. You ought to have a catalogue made by an expert. I'd be glad to recommend one. Yours is a fabulous collection, Marchesa. I must thank you for a memorable experience.'

Evidently Luigino got wind of these offers, for when Carrie decided to have a catalogue compiled he hastened to remind her that the pictures were family heirlooms which could never be exported. In the meantime she commissioned her old friend Reggie Temple to make copies of her favourites, much to Luigino's vexation.

When Italy entered the Second World War Carrie's assets in England and Canada were frozen. Though she resisted the temptation to sell her Primitives Attilio was an intermediary in the furtive sale of silver to defray the rising cost of her establishment. For household requirements she could draw on the country estates, supplemented by luxuries from the black

14

market. Her chef excelled himself in maintaining his high standard when provisions were scarce. Gradually her more precious works of art were removed to villas which seemed remote from the ravages of war. When German officers were billeted on the town palace she migrated to what she called her dower-house in the hills near Lucca, a vast manor with a baroque façade off the beaten track. Lack of petrol confined her there with her greyhounds and cockatoos while Monsignor Vaya stayed on in the palace, acting as interpreter for the German officers on whom he kept a wary eye to curb their acquisitive instincts.

When the allies reached Florence in August 1944 Carrie longed to be there to welcome them, but Attilio restrained her with a grisly account of conditions in the city. Off Limits signs had been posted on the palazzo but most of the windows had gone when the bridges were blown up and there was neither water nor electricity. With realistic relish he described the shattered sewers and gas mains, the rotting corpses under mounds of rubble beside the stagnant Arno, while German batteries continued to shell the town from Fiesole and hidden snipers picked off civilians. He had heard it all from the partisans he had met. The stifling heat and ubiquitous stench — not to mention the thousands of mosquitoes — created an Inferno.

'I feel it is my duty to go back all the same,' said Carrie.

'Between two opposing armies? It would be folly. The Campanile of Giotto has been hit, and all the bridges gone save the Ponte Vecchio. The shells are still whistling over the palazzo. It is my duty to prevent you from taking such a risk.'

So Carrie was forced to linger at her dower-house, for once feeling helpless and bored, while the rain of September poured steadily into the roofless buildings of Florence and the Arno began to swell.

In October — oh joy of joys! — an allied jeep drove up to the villa. Carrie's old friend Cecil Hobart, a former Florentine resident now a captain of the Allied Control Commission, had come with a colleague to see if she were safe. He explained that his job was to help the protection of Florentine masterpieces and 'of course you are first on our list.'

Carrie embraced him. 'You absolute angel! We've all been waiting for you gallant boys to rescue us. I feel like the Sleeping Princess just woken up. Now that you have found me you must stay. There are plenty of masterpieces here for your protection. Who's your cute colleague? He makes me wish I was younger.'

'*You* are the masterpiece, Carrie, you haven't changed in all these years. My colleague is Lieutenant Billington who has written a book on Beccafumi.'

'I shall expect you for dinner as well as luncheon, and bring your driver. You look tired and hungry.'

'Could we have a bath beforehand? That is what we need most.'

After their ablutions a substantial meal was served with vintage champagne that Attilio had put aside for the liberation. To the liberators this seemed, as indeed it was, a precarious oasis of pre-war tranquility. The cellars had been used as a deposit for over a hundred paintings from local museums and churches which Hobart and Billington examined with exclamations of wonder. When they felt obliged to return to their salvage operations in the city Carrie begged them to take her along with them. 'We'll come as soon as your palace is ready to receive you. Being a national monument it is Out of Bounds but there is neither light nor water and the windows are boarded up. Just now the neighbourhood is horribly unhygienic, bulldozers everywhere . . .'

'I long to get back into circulation.'

'You can't compete with the bulldozers, Carrie. I implore you to be patient. We can't thank you enough for this taste of civilization.'

'Promise to let me know when my palace is habitable.'

'We'll do our best to get it ship-shape. First we must find some glaziers for the windows.'

Attilio was given a lift to Florence to see things for himself and he returned a few days later in deep dejection. True, the palazzo was intact and the rooms had not been looted, but the floors were heaped with broken glass and everything was densely coated with dust. It would take an age to restore the *status quo*. The porter's family on the ground floor were still dazed and terrified by the shells and explosions and the women were slightly hysterical. Crawling from door to door, it had taken them half a day to find some drinking water, but Captain Hobart had distributed abundant army rations and they were grateful for the provisions Attilio had brought. Already they had set to work with brooms and buckets and some refugees had been engaged to help. The Marchesa must be patient. *Chi va piano va sano . . .*

Thanks to her friends of the Allied Control Commission Attilio made frequent trips by jeep to prepare the Amidei palace for Carrie's return. By the spring she was installed with some of her former splendour. She had begun to receive food parcels from America and their contents were transformed by her chef. The young officers she entertained knew nothing about her except that she had a historic title and a rollicking sense of humour. They regarded her as a dear dodo who was loads of fun; a few were disconcerted by such confidences as: 'All my husbands were stallions, though I never had a child. I think I shall adopt one, or even two, to keep me company in the evening of life. But one hears that it will soon be all over between men and women. It sounds rather dull to me but I guess I'm old-fashioned.'

Proud of her American origin, Carrie wanted to show that she remained a democrat. Many brought their girl-friends, and she introduced them to Luigi's great-nieces, a bewitching bevy of teenagers with flashing eyes. A tray of assorted drinks was always at hand while somebody strummed on the piano. Flirtation was encouraged and several became engaged. It seemed years since she had talked so much in her own language. She reminisced about the First World War when she

17

had entertained wounded officers from Gallipoli. They had been so unaccustomed to the freedom of Florentine conversation (meaning her own) that they had followed her female guests to their bedrooms and tried to rape them. The officers who visited her now were better behaved, but were they as virile? There was much to be said for virility, so long as it was kept under control . . . Carrie tended to repeat herself without realizing it, returning, ever and anon, to the plumber of Leigh and the young fellow called Grant, 'who was made like the Sensitive Plant', interspersed with personal comments. Her guests listened with amused bewilderment till she fell asleep. When she woke up they had vanished.

Her thoughts reverted to the children she had planned to adopt. Why keep greyhounds, pekinese and parrots when there were orphans crying for a home? Since the war they must have multiplied . . . But she wanted no dribbling tiny tots or sticky little girls: they would have to be boys of eight or nine whose development would be worth watching: if they were clever she would give them an English education, send them to Eton perhaps to give them polish. She urged Attilio to look for a decent family with superfluous mouths to feed, for she disliked the abstract idea of an orphanage.

Attilio's response was not optimistic. He tried to laugh it off as another of Carrie's caprices. 'People will presume that they are the fruit of some tender indiscretion,' he told her.

'All the better. It will take years off my age, and it will brighten up the atmosphere. The palace is too full of sad memories.'

'It does credit to your charitable heart, Signora Marchesa, but have you considered the domestic complications? Personally I do not mind the extra work but the others will. The chef is already sufficiently temperamental, complaining of his varicose veins, always a warning that he is about to give notice. And if he goes, the maids will follow. I fear we shall have no more peace, Signora Marchesa.'

Opposition only made Carrie more stubborn. She applied

to Monsignor Vaya, who recommended an orphanage near the monastery where he was staying. Carrie brought a generous hamper of sweetmeats for the children and explained her mission to the priest in charge, a kindly bespectacled soul with children clinging to his cassock. He led them through dreary schoolrooms to a noisy back yard where a football was being kicked about. Together they inspected a dozen little boys of different sizes, asking them if they would like to live with the Marchesa in the city. All except two were silent and abashed, as if such a prospect alarmed them. The two who stepped forward were bright-eyed brothers called Italo and Orlando, and they gazed at Carrie as if she were a fairy godmother.

When they kissed her she remarked: 'They are simply adorable. I have never been so flattered in my life. This is love at first sight!' She wanted to take them immediately but for this she would have to obtain the director's permission and the director was absent. 'I cannot assume the responsibility,' the priest told her, 'though I'm sure he will be glad to establish them in so distinguished a home.'

After negotiations with Monsignor Vaya Carrie's adoption of Italo and Orlando was arranged. All too soon for Attilio's comfort Carrie went to fetch them from the orphanage, which they left without shedding a tear. To be driven in an Isotta Fraschini was a thrilling new experience for them and they screamed with delight on the short journey to the palazzo, nor did their excitement diminish on arrival. Carrie's dogs and cockatoos greeted them with loud yappings and squawkings but their cacophony was a trifle compared with that of the newcomers, who ran from room to room like a couple of wild Indians. Carrie did not seem to mind: their antics amused her as much as they distressed Attilio, who looked on with an 'I told you so' expression. Orlando, the younger of the two, was the more mischievous and Italo followed his lead. Together they raided the larder, breaking into pots of honey and preserves, and their table manners were barbaric, as if they were unaccustomed to knives and forks and napkins. As for cleanliness, they quickly defeated the effect of a good scrubbing.

A religious tutor, Don Placido, was engaged to educate them, and he reported that Italo was a zealous and attentive pupil, but Orlando was unruly and difficult. He hoped that Italo's example would be followed. But it was Orlando who became Carrie's favourite. He would rush into her bedroom to cover her with wet kisses. Already he saw himself in the role of seductive male, flattering her outrageously. '*Come sei bella, Mammina, bella bella bella. Ti voglio tanto bene sai. Dammi un bacino. Ancora, ancora!*' And Carrie melted in his muscular little arms: '*Che birichino!*'

While visiting him in his bath Carrie had been impressed by his physique, for he was proud to display his precocious development. Italo, though older, was far less well-endowed: he was also shy. From this observation Carrie drew certain conclusions. Italo would become a scholar, Orlando an athlete. Don Placido agreed with her. Though Carrie tried to be impartial there could be no doubt that Orlando had won her heart. His naughtiness was attributed to healthy high spirits, as when he killed her prized cockatoo.

Such a beautiful bird, he fancied, would make a succulent roast, and its feathers would embellish one of the Marchesa's hats. After throttling it he had taken it down to the kitchen to be plucked. The chef was so angry that he slapped the boy's face. 'You little monster,' he shouted, 'the Marchesa will be heartbroken; she was devoted to that bird. Anyhow it was at least fifty years old and cockatoos are not edible. The kitchen is my domain, and I won't have you snooping into my larder. Several pots of jam have been missing and I can guess who's to blame. Now run off and apologise for your misdeed, and don't you dare show your mug in here again!'

Crestfallen, Orlando sought refuge in the garage, where he had made friends with Dante the chauffeur. Dante laughed at his tearful tale and gave him a spin in the Isotta Fraschini, allowing him to take over the wheel in the Cascine, which gave him a pleasurable sense of domination. Dante was the only member of Carrie's staff who took a fancy to him. Orlando felt more at home in the garage, where every gadget appealed to his devouring curiosity. The smell of petrol was incense to his nostrils; already he longed for the day when he could drive his own car.

Carrie readily forgave the destruction of her pet cockatoo, and Orlando boasted to Italo that he could do what he pleased with the old lady. On shopping expeditions she paid marked attention to Orlando's preferences, for unlike Italo he was very sure of his taste. He would insist on inspecting every article in the shop: sweaters, shirts, socks, shoes were pulled down from shelves and tested for size and comfort, often to be discarded with, 'That would do for Italo', or, surveying himself in a looking-glass, 'It is not exactly my style.' For a boy of eleven he was remarkably self-assured.

Carrie would send for the boys after dinner to exhibit them to her guests, but whereas Italo was too shy to appear — he was said to be studying, 'a regular bookworm' — Orlando shone on such occasions. The ladies could not resist caressing such a cunning little cherub. They offered him lumps of sugar dipped in their coffee and crammed him with *marrons glacés*.

Attilio watched Carrie's latest infatuation with growing concern. He called Orlando 'the Delinquent' and prophesied that he would come to no good. Since Don Placido had attempted in vain to control him Orlando accused him of 'doing shameful things' with Italo during lessons. Though this was untrue the tutor was dismissed and the boys were sent to a co-educational day-school under Anglo-American management where English, French and German were also taught. Their absence improved Attilio's temper, which had recently shown signs of exasperation.

The timid and studious Italo soon carried off several school prizes. Already he evinced such a gift for languages that Carrie was advised to send him to Switzerland for a special course of

21

training in the technique of hotel administration. But Orlando was expelled for exposing himself once too often to the girls. Silly bitches, he said, not to appreciate their luck! Carrie pleaded for him with the director; it seemed such a harmless peccadillo...But the director had received too many complaints. He was extremely sorry but Orlando was giving the school a bad name. Parents would remove their daughters if he was allowed to stay on. Besides he was insubordinate — a bad example to others.

What was Carrie to do with her darling? She appealed to Attilio. 'Send him to an institution for juvenile delinquents, Signora Marchesa. If you keep him here your entire staff will abandon you.'

' Even you, Attilio?'

'Even me: you must choose between us.'

This was sheer blackmail, for she could not envisage her future without Attilio. In a frightening flash she realized how much she had depended on him all these decades. He, too, was getting older, and age was curdling his temper. She had taken him too much for granted. Obviously, he was jealous of Orlando. What a bore. Her pet would have to be sacrificed, but how? She prayed fervently in the family chapel for a happy solution.

Cecil Hobart, now a remnant of the Allied Control Commission, helped her to find one. A film-producing friend of his was recruiting protagonists for a romanticized version of Leonardo da Vinci's 'life and loves', and so far had failed to find a juvenile Leonardo. It occurred to Cecil, as his artistic consultant, that Orlando possessed the physical qualifications. He spoke of this to Carrie. Could he bring Ted Henniker to the palazzo?

'Orlando has never acted in his life. He is a child of nature.'

'All the better. Ted has a marvellous director with several stars to his credit, discovered and moulded by himself. He prefers to pick them raw. Micky Montana and Hermione Devlin were his latest finds. Micky was a taxi driver and

Hermoine a typist. Look where they are now, reaping in the shekels. Orlando's just the right age . . .'

The idea was so novel to Carrie, who knew nothing about films, that it appealed to her sense of fantasy. She took an instant liking to Ted Henniker, a jovial puff-ball of a man, who brought her a peach-fed Virginia ham to remind her of 'the old country' and a huge box of chocolate marshmallows. Orlando was told nothing about the project and Ted Henniker had a chance to study him before, during, and after a spectacular 'Escoffier' dinner, since rumour of the great film had got round to the kitchen. Henniker was impressed. Not only was the boy photogenic but there was something consciously dramatic about him, preoccupied with the effect he was producing. When he cuddled the Marchesa one eye was on the guests. Ted Henniker asked him: 'Would you like to come to America?'

'It has always been my dream. But I don't want to leave the Marchesa. She must come with us.'

'We shall see.'

Ted was a quick operator: his photographers arrived with cinecameras on the morrow to take shots of Orlando in every conceivable pose, and he so enjoyed being the centre of attention that he collaborated with the photographers and exerted all his impudent charm. 'Do you want me to undress?' he asked. 'You should see my gorgeous muscles.' So they took a few shots of him in the nude turning cartwheels and posing as Michelangelo's David. 'That kid's okay,' they told Carrie. 'We guess he'll be another Valentino.'

Carrie was delighted. 'I've adopted a future film star,' she told her friends. Before she knew it she was signing a contract with Ted Henniker, who paid her an enormous cheque in advance. Of course, there was no question of her accompanying him to Hollywood. She entrusted him to Ted, who promised him a Rolls Royce if he behaved.

'Why are all my clocks silent, Attilio? It must be a century since I last heard them ticking.'

'You commanded them to be stopped, Signora Marchesa.

You complained of the noise they made and you said the church-bells were sufficient.'

'Did I really? Well, do get them started again. Send for the clock man, the old fellow with the wall eye who stank of garlic.'

'Alas, he is no longer with us, Marchesa. But I can wind them myself.'

'You are a wonder, Attilio, you could wind anything!'

Surrounded by blown-up photographs of Orlando in the nude, the Marchesa Carrie died quietly in her sleep.

All Florence trooped into the frescoed hall where she lay in state before the coffin closed over her. She was dressed as for a ball in a long silver lamé gown with a silver fillet binding her faded gold hair, a mother o' pearl rosary between her folded hands. Her face had been so made up that it was like a wax doll's. 'Pure Fabergé!' exclaimed Cecil Hobart. By the light of flickering candles her hands seemed transparent. Wreaths of lilies and stacks of tuberoses embowered the bier. Carrie would have approved of the décor.

'Attilio's last gala,' snarled the Marchese Luigino with a sour grimace.

Leo's Ivory Tower

'One has to visit museums to see pictures which were not painted for museums. Private collections, like mine, are doomed. All will end up in public picture wards. Fortunately, I'll be cremated by then . . .'

Listening to him, looking at him, you would never suspect that Leo Kremer had originated in Brooklyn. Brooklyn was his source of worldly wealth. Germany was the land of his ancestors, but Harvard had given him a Bostonian veneer, an almost English drawl. He tended to speak in paradoxes with a whimsical smile and it was difficult to tell when he was serious. His pale grey eyes watched one intently, as if to test the effect of a theory which sounded startling. But he scrutinised works of art more closely than human beings, and he could discern beauty where others failed to perceive it.

He had come to Florence in the eighteen-nineties and fallen in love, not only with its artistic treasures but with its sounds and smells — the shrill cries of street-hawkers and the mellow pealing of church-bells, the musty effluvia of wine-shops and the pungent exhalations of kitchens — above all with its stones, the rusticated blocks of severe substantial palaces mottled and modelled by sunlight and moonlight, and the carved lintels over doorways and windows.

As soon as he graduated from Harvard he chose to perch in a medieval tower near the Ponte Vecchio, and he migrated from one tower to another till he decided to build one of his own — attached to a house which was called the Torre di Leo. He had intended to become an art historian, but his nature was contemplative and he lacked academic ambition. In spite of his exceptional knowledge of Italian painting and sculpture he had little incentive to propagate it, but when he discovered a forgotten fresco or bas-relief he would draw the attention of scholars to it in some esoteric publication. A fluent, if hesitant, speaker, it cost him a disproportionate effort to formulate his ideas in writing. Pacing up and down his study, he always wrote standing at a fifteenth-century lectern. The sporadic articles he produced after weeks of peripatetic gestation were so packed with parentheses that they were as abstruse as metaphysical essays. One had to read every sentence twice over and then, apart from the dates and place-names, one was none too sure of its meaning. 'They tell me I write like Henry James,' he would say. 'I appreciate the compliment though, unlike the average art historian, I cannot produce plausible fiction.'

Leo spent much of his time in antique shops and, under the illusion that he was incognito, he wore his oldest, shabbiest clothes on these occasions. There was an élite of international art dealers in Florence at the turn of the century and these were his boon companions. His rooms were crammed with the spoils of his excursions and objects he had taken on approval, for he wanted to ascertain that he could live with what had spontaneously caught his fancy. With so dependable a client the dealers dared not expostulate if he changed his mind and sent an object back. 'It is like taking a mistress or a wife,' he used to say. So far he had taken neither: his natural vocation was that of a bachelor. Most of the ladies he consorted with were intellectuals, angular and earnest. Their garments imitated those of the Cinquecento and their hair was bound with Botticellian fillets. The feminists were distinctly mannish in their attire. Leo's relations with them were playfully professorial. They followed him round the galleries and argued with him, a little breathlessly, about the texture of a Titian and the contours of a Pontormo. 'The sultan and his harem,' it was said.

Everybody in Florence had to be credited with a lover, however incongruous, and there was an unfounded rumour that Leo had a penchant for peasant girls. But he was totally dedicated to his art collection, content with his acquisitions and the problems of attribution which varied from day to day. His taste was as eclectic as it was precious: every object was the cream of its kind. Yet he had no talent for arrangement: he was the antithesis of an interior decorator. The Renaissance tables and chests that monopolized his rooms were solid and austere. His maiolica vases and Venetian bowls were innocent of flowers. The feminine touch was lacking, not for want of women in the house. Corinna, an elderly maid, looked after him like a governess and her sister Assunta prepared his simple meals. They shared his jokes and were on the best of terms. In their private view all foreigners were a bit loony. It suited them to serve an easy-going bachelor. His lady friends never impinged on his domestic habits.

While he enjoyed showing his treasures to initiates, Leo was never known to offer them a meal. A discussion of his latest 'find' was usually prolonged in some neighbouring café. He was un-American in his indifference to comfort and he kept aloof from fashionable society, from the Marchesas and Contessas who longed to peep at his collection, if only to disparage it. 'I prefer to converse with my cook,' he said. 'Assunta has never studied art but I trust her judgement. She knows instinctively if a picture is worth buying. She will cross herself and say: "Beautiful, the Blessed Madonna!" or, "*Con rispetto parlando*, that's just a trollop!" "Those are the hills of Mugello", or "Who ever imagined such a crazy landscape? That painter must have been drunk." Fundamentally, she is right.'

When he decided to build his tower at Arcetri Leo relished the endless discussion of plans — he always had a new one — with his masons, carpenters, joiners and plasterers, whom he regarded as lineal survivors of the Renaissance. Their Tuscan aspirates and pungent locutions enchanted him. He was his own architect, and as he changed his mind frequently the result was peculiar. 'The Florentines avoid dull symmetry — it

27

is one of their virtues,' he maintained. Consequently the entrance was in an inconspicuous corner behind the building. From an octagonal vestibule you descended into a spacious 'minstrels' gallery.' Bedrooms and bathrooms were sporadic afterthoughts. Leo's study was accommodated in the tower with a magnificent view from every window. The main structure became larger than he had anticipated, spreading into an irregular pile that defied exact description. In a strange way it came to resemble Leo's personality.

As the building expanded Leo amassed more and more furniture, and it occurred to him that the place required additional bipeds to enliven it. He began to regret that his circle of friends was restricted. All of them were elderly or looked older than their years. His next of kin were indigenous to Wall Street: they regarded Leo as the wayward genius of the family, and it was thanks to them that his investments flourished. Nothing could tempt them to depraved and decadent Europe. They were rabid isolationists who considered it unpatriotic to live abroad though they had an enormous cousinship in Germany, for whose salient efficiency and moral worth they made an exception.

Leo suddenly remembered these cousins whom he had not seen for ages. They had intellectual hobbies outside their business, and all were intensely musical. Eugen played the harpsichord, Mitzi the harp, and the children were said to make up a creditable string quartet. Why not invite them to his Florentine tower? He had bought a decorative spinet and a viola da gamba, more for their shapes than their sounds, and he mentioned these in his invitation to 'the land where the citrons bloom.'

Eugen and Mitzi were unable to leave their emporium but they accepted eagerly on behalf of Kurt and Hedwig, their eldest children. Kurt was twenty-two, still studying law; Hedwig, or Hedy, was just eighteen. From the snapshots enclosed in Mitzi's letter Kurt looked truly Teutonic with his close-cropped skull in some sort of uniform; Hedy, well, like many a grinning *backfisch*. No hint of a synagogue in either of them: they evoked the savour of sauerkraut. Yet, like himself, they were descended from a line of rabbis. Hedy's juvenile vivacity might compensate for plainness of feature. The snapshots were rather blurred. Come what may, the experiment seemed worth risking. He looked forward to showing them his Florence.

No doubt Kurt would find his own bearings. Leo's female acquaintances would help him to cope with Hedy if he found her difficult. Mable Crudding had run a girls' finishing school before devoting herself to the works of Sodoma; Gloria Heap adored all things German and spoke the language like a native; Loelia Kitson could play duets with her and introduce her to Dante. At a pinch he might entrust her to Amanda Dolphin who was bound to introduce her to Sappho. It was too long since he had had contacts with the younger generation. Perhaps at forty-six it was too late . . .

Corinna and Assunta were excited by the prospect of house-guests for a change. They had prevailed on Leo to engage their nieces Renata and Ada as the place was far too big for so limited a staff. They were plump and pretty and exceedingly vociferous. Leo insisted on dressing them in old-fashioned peasant costumes with flowery aprons and silk kerchiefs on their piled-up hair. He bought them tambourines and encouraged them to dance the tarantella and sing *stornelli* after dinner. So pleasantly was he entertained by the frolics of these handmaidens that he began to regret inviting his distant cousins.

The arrival of Kurt and Hedwig created a novel commotion at Leo's tower. Kurt's gorilla handshake was crushing, but Hedy flung her arms round Leo's neck and her kisses, equally unexpected, soothed his agony. Albeit no beauty, she was an improvement on her snapshot: her expression brightened when she talked, and she had much to say about the journey, the friendly Italians who shared their compartment on the train and offered them wine and salami, the glimpse of the

Leaning Tower — ('I'm so glad your tower does not lean!'), — the picturesque drive from the station, the bridges over the Arno, and so forth. She emitted little yelps when he showed her her room and the view from the balcony. 'Oh, I am so happy to be here. It is much lovelier than my premonitions. Thank you, oh thank you, for inviting your unknown cousins.'

She sat down at the spinet and played Beethoven's 'Bagatelle for Elisa' while Kurt went off to shave. *'Come suona bene, la Signorina,'* said Corinna, who stood listening at the door with a tray of cakes and a decanter of *vin santo*. Hedy had brought what the place had been lacking — music and feminine company for the *Signore*. The frumps who usually called on him — what purgatory! — could not be considered feminine. Leo was exhilarated by the difference. He had never been hugged and embraced so often before.

In the churches and museums to which Leo felt obliged to conduct his young cousins Kurt made no effort to stifle his yawns, and even Hedy thought Leo's raptures exaggerated after the first week. When he proposed to open her eyes to the virility of Masaccio she said: 'Why not stay at home? I am quite happy to bask amid the fragrance of your wistaria. Do you never relax, Cousin Leo? Must you always be rushing in and out of antique shops? Come, I will play for you, and perhaps you will be moved to sing.' But Leo was neither a tenor nor a baritone: he had no voice for singing. He preferred the idea of music to the reality. The names of the great composers rolled easily off his tongue. As he said, they were so evocative. One immediately wanted to dance a minuet to the name of Mozart and a waltz to that of Strauss. Hedy tried to make him sing *Du bist die Ruh*. He could remember the words from his childhood but the voice was so flat that both of them burst out laughing.

'I feel already the benefit of this air,' she told him.

'Yes, it is what gives the Florentines their keen wit and clear vision.'

'I find it soporific,' said Kurt. 'All the same I have a ravenous appetite. Is it time for lunch? My mouth waters for *ravioli*.'

Kurt left them to themselves while he borrowed a bicycle to explore the countryside. The open air cafés were what he most enjoyed, and he soon found congenial compatriots to swim with and go boating on the Arno and riding in the Cascine. He also discovered a fencing school where he could indulge his favourite exercise. His independence suited Leo, who privately thought him a nuisance. His attempts to flirt with Renata and Ada had met with rebuffs and Assunta had complained of him to Leo. Apparently the crudity of his advances had alarmed them. Had he been gentler they might have been flattered. Both girls were engaged to boys with better manners. He grew sullen after this repulse and Leo was relieved when he had to return to Düsseldorf.

Hedy begged to stay on. 'I don't want to go home,' she cried, 'I'm enjoying it far too much here.' Kurt wanted her to travel with him — she was so young for her age — but Cousin Leo was an innocuous old fogey, and he knew plenty of matrons to chaperon her if necessary.

As soon as Kurt left with his portmanteau full of gimcrack souvenirs Hedy flung her arms round Leo and exclaimed: 'At last we are together! Kurt was jealous of our friendship. For a brother he is tiresomely possessive. It was not easy to persuade him to let me stay. I told him not to be selfish. At home I scrub and sew and do the housework, and this is my first real holiday. Here everything is divine, and you are an absolute darling. Forget about your age, it doesn't matter. Kiss me — no, not like that — a proper kiss on the lips.'

Leo needed no further prompting as she pressed her lissome body against his and slipped her pointed tongue into his mouth. His knees trembled, his head swam. Quite a novel sensation. 'Do you never sunbathe, Leo?' she asked him. 'Your terrace is ideal for sunbathing.'

'Too busy for that kind of thing and too bony. Besides, it would shock the maids.'

Hedy giggled. 'All the better!'

In no time she tripped on to the terrace in her dressing-gown with a mattress and some pillows. 'Be an angel and fetch me some olive oil,' she pleaded. And in no time she was stretched stark naked in the sun with a voluptuous sigh. Coyly she asked Leo to spread some oil over her neck and arms. While pouring it his hands were emboldened to caress her bosom and belly. Far from remonstrating, she murmured 'Delicious!' closing her eyes with a seraphic smile as he massaged her loins. 'Do go on!' Leo's fingers seemed to catch fire as they tightened round her mound of Venus and dabbled in wisps of moist hair. 'I feel like Benvenuto Cellini,' he said. 'What glorious curves to mould!'

He was making a fresh discovery about himself instead of the Old Masters. Surrounded by intellectuals who had repressed their sexual instincts, his relations with women had been platonic, he had neglected his body. Now he became conscious of an attraction to this creature whose mind meant nothing to him. He congratulated himself on his ability to rouse her, as the tautening of her bosom testified. 'Go on,' she repeated. 'You are a fine masseur.'

Leo blinked and withdrew his oily hand with a sheepish grimace. Supposing the maids were peeping? This was altogether too public. 'You make me forget my age. I am but human.'

'You should sunbathe also. It would do you good. You are too pale.'

As he drew himself up from his kneeling position, a little dizzy, Hedy clung to him. 'Another kiss!' But Renata was coming to call him to the telephone. 'Cover yourself quickly,' he whispered. As if to tantalize him, she refused to budge. Renata's face flushed crimson. *'Scostumata!'* she muttered. Leo explained to her that the cult of nudity was quite respectable in Germany — she mustn't be shocked. *'Ma che vergogna!'* Leo chuckled at her embarrassment but he was annoyed that the telephone should have interrupted his fun.

Sunbathing melted the thin ice, as it were, between the juvenile Hedwig and her middle-aged cousin. She soon

32

persuaded him to lie shirtless beside her on the terrace, though she could not induce him to shed his trousers. Her primitive innocence and naïve prattle beguiled him like a Schubert song — such a contrast with the pedantic spinsters he had cultivated in the past.

After a fortnight of intensive sightseeing Hedy candidly confessed that she had had a surfeit of picture galleries. 'I am quite content at stay at home, for I feel this is my spiritual home, Cousin Leo. Why leave this heavenly house and garden? Everything is perfect here.'

It annoyed her that she could not keep him away from the antique shops. 'Haven't you enough treasures to satisfy you? Don't you ever feel crushed by them? Must you go on and on collecting? I wish you would add me to your collection. I think I would improve it, a live specimen from Düsseldorf, guaranteed virginal, *nicht wahr?*'

While he reverted to his former routine Hedy spent hours practising on the Steinway grand he had procured, for her secret ambition was to become a concert pianist. Already a skilled performer, she practised with such concentration that she failed to notice when he crept beside her with a box of *pralinés*. Since her arrival she forgot about time. Though her parents urged her to return, her life with Leo was so blissfully carefree that she had no desire to obey them. They also wrote to Leo thanking him for all his kindness to their beloved Hedwig, who must have outstayed her welcome. 'We miss her and we fear she is growing lazy as she never writes. We are also worried about the Italians she may meet. How can you protect our ewe-lamb from the Latin wolves? She is too young to be left alone — even with you, dear Leo. After all, you are a bachelor . . .'

Leo replied that she seemed able to look after herself. It would be a pity to recall her when she was acquiring essential knowledge of history and art. Moreover, she was making great progress with the pianoforte. Florence was the best of finishing schools . . .

As the weather grew hotter Hedy wandered about the house

barefoot in her dressing-gown. She entered Leo's room without knocking and sat on his bed while he shaved, twiddling her bare toes and manicuring her nails. Leo was titillated by these intimacies. He took her out driving in his new Fiat to Siena, Arezzo, and Assisi. The frescoes he showed her with erudite commentaries made less impression than the white oxen and other details of Tuscan scenery, which at any rate gave her a hearty appetite. After a copious meal in a *trattoria* with glass upon glass of red Chianti she gazed at Leo with a kittenish expression and said: 'You make me feel naughty. Do you feel the same?' She dozed off in the car, nestling against his shoulder, and he had much ado to restrain his mischievous fingers.

Another appeal from Düsseldorf awaited her at the tower. 'What am I to do?' she cried. 'I'd love to stay here for ever but Papa commands me to go home. He threatens to stop my allowance. And Kurt says it is your fault, that your influence is dangerous.'

'Of course you are free to stay as long as you like, never mind about the allowance. But I don't want to be a bone of contention. Perhaps you ought to go. Evidently they need you.'

Hedy wailed: 'How can you be so callous? Have I meant so little to you?' Tears began rolling out of her eyes. 'Don't send me back to them. Let me stay with you. Can't you realize how fond of you I have grown, Leo? I forget we happen to be cousins — we are already so much closer to each other.'

Leo was strangely disconcerted. He had a vague suspicion of being ambushed. What had he let himself in for? Hedy was putting him in a position whose implications began to alarm him. So far he had only been serious about works of art. Again she threw her arms round his neck and covered him with kisses. 'This will not do, Hedy. I'm too old. I could almost be your father.'

'Be my father, please! I ask for nothing better. I'll be your loving daughter.'

34

So Hedy stayed on and on and Leo played a game of hide and seek with her. He hid among the antique shops where she could not find him, and he listened absent-mindedly to her prattle, for he thought he had made a sensational discovery.

In a back yard among heaped fragments of stonework, he had come across a rusty bronze horse lying on its flank. At a glance he recognized it as a sixteenth-century production, perhaps even earlier. Despite his eagerness to buy it he tried to conceal his trepidation by haggling for it nonchalantly. When the dealer was unwilling to climb down he proposed a round sum for the inclusion of a pedestal and some dilapidated cherubs. The dealer was stubborn, and Leo had to wait on tenterhooks until he could clinch the bargain for a trifling reduction to save face. The bronze horse obsessed him to such a degree that he scarcely noticed Hedy. When the bullock cart unloaded its heavy burden Leo helped to unpack it and carry it into his vestibule. During the next few days, armed with soap and brushes, he gradually removed the coating of dirt and rust while Hedy looked on in a pet. 'Would you like to borrow my face cream?' she asked mockingly. Leo sweated with excitement as the masterly modelling of mane and muzzle, of raised forelegs and fetlocks, glowed as in a paddock: he was reminded of the Colleoni monument at Venice and the Gattamelata at Padua, and the horses of St Mark's pranced before his dazzled vision. He stood and sat beside it, he walked round it, thrilled as he had never been by any live horse. 'Yes, it is a genuine gee-gee and no mistake,' said Assunta with approval. 'We shall soon hear its whinnying all over the house.' Hedy was less enthusastic than the housemaids. She felt she had a rival with which she could not compete.

Once it was settled on its marble pedestal it dominated the vestibule like a Derby winner. Leo returned to feast his eyes on it, sometimes in the middle of a meal. He could talk of little else. Photographers were summoned to make studies of it from every angle and an egg-nog party was given in its honour. The art historians, led by Dr Max Hussander who had published two stout volumes on Renaissance sculpture, were invited to inspect it. They approached it in a solemn group with varied exclamations in English, French and Italian. They examined it minutely in silence and watched each other keenly for a cue. That it was a model for an equestrian monument went without saying, but whose? Leo had his private theory, but he hoped that somebody would corroborate it.

Dr Hussander seldom revealed his opinion until a colleague ventured to express one. After a prolonged scrutiny on tiptoe with a magnifying glass he barked: 'An absolute stunner, by Jove!' *'C'est formidable, une vraie trouvaille,'* gasped Professor Bernichon. *'Mi sembra un capolavoro,'* added Dr Piazzani. 'Assuredly it shows Paduan influence. The name of Andrea Riccio occurs to me first.' 'I see what you mean: the springing movement of his horse in the V. and A. But to my eye it looks like — well, wait for my next book on Italian bronzes. The whole question is thrashed out there for good and all.'

'My vote is for Riccio, the curly-haired,' said Mabel Crudding, 'but as you know I specialize in Sodoma. What fun if they knew each other! I'll dream of it tonight . . .'

Losing patience, Leo broke in: 'Seriously, doesn't it remind you of Leonardo's drawings at Windsor?'

'That is precisely what I was thinking,' said Professor Bernichon. 'The Trivulzio monument.'

'Or the Sforza,' said Leo. 'I hesitated to pronounce so bold an attribution but now that Professor Bernichon of the Louvre has spoken, the more I observe it the more convinced I become that it must be by the hand of Leonardo.' He produced reproductions of Leonardo's drawings for comparison.

'I should esteem it a favour if you would grant me permission to publish it,' said the French professor. 'It will cause a prodigious sensation. I should date it between 1511 and 1512 when Gian Giacomo Trivulzio governed Milan with Gaston de Foix after the death of Charles d'Amboise.'

'Of course, of course,' said Leo, 'though I was inclined to date it somewhat earlier.'

36

'In view of my previous publications,' interposed Dr Hussander, 'I have a prior claim.'

While the experts were bickering Hedy put her tongue out at the horse and wrinkled up her nose. So much hocus-pocus, she thought resentfully. 'You all think and talk too much about art,' she said. 'What about life? Come and eat some plum cake. I've been trying to make the place cosier, but what can one do with Leo? When I put flowers in the vases he throws them out — I mean the flowers.'

She had in fact filled Leo's rarest maiolica vases with pink gladioli and Leo had made a scene. 'I forbid you to touch my antiques,' he snapped at her.

'But the flowers are alive — they have the beauty of the living,' she protested.

'You have yet to understand the superior beauty of fifteenth-century maiolica. Flowers fade beside the lustre of Faenza: they are a vulgar intrusion.'

'I only hoped to please you. Perhaps I had better go back to Düsseldorf,' she whimpered.

'Yes, you had better go.'

This was the first time she had seen Leo in a temper and she recoiled from him in dismay while he glared at her with hatred.

She had no intention of leaving him, however. The same night she crept into his bed and begged him to forgive her. The contact of her bare body weakened his resolve to let her go. She wound herself round him like a cobra — if cobras were warm-blooded. Her musky odour affected him as an aphrodisiac and melted his will to resist her. She was astonishingly fertile in expedients, versatile, even vicious with her teeth. Her nails dug into his back. Consummation was inevitable before he fell asleep.

'I have given you my all,' she told him when he awoke with her arms still round him. He was aware of pins and needles in his legs. Her armpits stifled him.

'Your all?' he gasped. 'Explain yourself, Hedy.'

'I've given myself completely. I am no longer a virgin.'

'Nonsense, don't talk like a cheap novelette. I guess you lost your virginity in your cradle. All the same I congratulate you. To have seduced an old fogy like me is a feat any professional would be proud of.' *Post coitum* . . . he brooded.

Hedy was too outraged to speak. Such odious ingratitude! Huddled in an eddy of bedclothes, her nose looked swollen in a drawn white face. Leo handed her a looking-glass. 'Let me fetch you some powder. Your proboscis shines like a street-lamp. Are you really eighteen? I don't believe it.'

Her appearance was so repulsive that he forgot his own. He poured himself a glass of water and drank it at a gulp. 'Do run off and brush your teeth before the maids arrive. Gorgonzola has its merits, but not on the breath . . .'

Suddenly Hedy let out a piercing scream. Leo clapped a hand over her mouth and she bit it. Renata and Ada rushed in to see what was happening. 'The Signorina is having a fit,' Leo told them, and they decided that she required a good purge. 'And I need some disinfectant.' His hand was bleeding profusely. All their attention was concentrated on Leo. Assunta joined them with boric acid and bandages. *'Povero Signore! Ma com'è successo?'* Hedy might yell her head off as far as they were concerned.

II

'Has Leo had a stroke? He looks twenty years older.'

'The same as a stroke. He has married that minx of a cousin. Mark my words, it will be the death of him.'

'Poor old Leo. He must have been cornered. I wonder how it happened. The girl has nothing in common with him. Evidently she is more scheming than one suspected.'

'If only she were amiable. She is certain to turn into a shrew. Already he has the air of a hen-pecked husband. One's heart bleeds for him . . .'

Leo had been frightened into it by Hedwig's parents, who

accused him of compromising their daughter since she had refused to return to them. Even if she returned, her reputation was soiled. Marriage was the only possible form of reparation. Kurt would soon arrive in Florence with a solicitor to draw up a settlement, failing which he would challenge Leo to a duel. 'Only arms can satisfy the honour of our family,' he had written. 'I am ready to leave the choice of weapons to you but I warn you that I am as proficient with pistols as with swords ...'

The contingency of facing that oaf again depressed Leo. As for fighting a duel with him, the idea was preposterous. At the same time Hedy informed him tearfully that she was pregnant. Leo heard the news without apparent emotion but at heart he was not displeased. Though he was thoroughly tired of Hedy he felt he could endure a loveless match for the sake of an heir to his art collection. Her condition might account for the caprices that got on his nerves. When she was not practising her scales — a torment to which he had grown accustomed — she lay for hours on a deck-chair in the garden smoking endless cigarettes, knocking the ashes into the flower-bed and, indoors, on his priceless carpets. He preferred her scales to her conversation. She sat in Doney's eating chocolate eclairs and ice-cream while he shopped, but at tea parties she was apt to sulk in corners. She was not the type of girl to attract Italians when she ogled them and the maiden ladies who tried to entertain her as a favour to Leo soon washed their hands of her, for she never kept appointments or apologized for not doing so.

Leo's spirits rallied with the prospect of paternity, and Hedy jumped at a marriage which would release her from domestic drudgery and provide her with financial security. In many little ways she was more accommodating. She pretended to admire Leo's purchases; she even became reconciled to his bronze horse. 'It has the divine touch of Leonardo,' he heard her say. 'What muscle! What mastery!' She memorized Leo's remarks and repeated them to his various visitors, imitating his drawl, his fanciful epithets, his ironic laughter. She began to assume the role of a gracious chatelaine and to dream of a musical salon she would dominate.

Professor Bernichon's monograph on the Leonardo horse brought fresh flocks of amateurs to Leo's Tower who were impressed by Hedy's performance as a guide. Her memory of the names of early Tuscan artists even impressed Leo, who delegated to her the task of showing his collection. Pacino di Bonaguida, Lippo di Benivieni, the Master of Saint Cecilia, Maso di Banco, and a dozen more, tripped off her tongue with astonishing self-assurance. She waxed lyrical about the *putto*, the male infant who seemed to personify the Quattrocento. 'How he makes the air move!' she exlaimed. 'Note how Donatello swells his contours!'

'So do you,' said Leo. 'Let's put him in your bedroom. I hope our own *putto* will be as full of joy. We must think of a suitable name for him. Have you thought of one, Hedy?'

'Isn't it rather premature? Supposing it's a girl?'

'Better be prepared in either case.'

Since those threatening letters from her parents and Kurt's insolent challenge Leo refused to have any further dealings with them. Hedy did not care, for she realized that Leo was far more affluent than she had supposed. As an art collector he hated to spend money on superfluous luxuries but Hedy could coax him into extravagances he would not have tolerated as a bachelor. She revelled in the freedom she had gained at the cost of some physical discomfort. Corinna and Assunta took turns to nurse her tenderly during her confinement, respecting her slightest whim. Leo, who had a horror of the physical details, went off to Siena to revise certain attributions. He concealed his disappointment when, after an unusually protracted labour (and she had been eating like a horse till the eleventh hour), Hedy presented him with a diminutive daughter.

Hedy declared that she would not repeat the experience, her birth pangs had been too prolonged. The wailing of infants was as nerve-racking to Leo as it was to Hedy, and the baby, christened Lisa after Beethoven's friend, was entrusted to a buxom *balia,* or wet-nurse, with a copious supply of milk. A nanny goat was kept in reserve as a substitute. Leo stood aloof from the infant until she could toddle and sit on his knee.

Lisa grew rapidly and Leo pandered to her exhibitionistic instincts. 'Her baby-talk is far more amusing than Hedy's,' he averred. 'She does not say much, of course, but what she says is sensible and pragmatic. Her Italian is already fluent. *Pipï* and *popò* are so much prettier than the English words for the calls of nature. She is too young to appreciate art but she loves music. Play a little Bach for her, Hedy, let her dance!' And Lisa would jump up and down to the rhythm in a primitive jig. After a few whirls and twirls she would rush laughing towards Leo who caught her in his arms.

After a tour of Leo's collection his guests were offered refreshment in the minstrels' gallery and Lisa was invited to dance for them. Without further prompting she kicked off her slippers and improvised a solo to the music. '*Bravissima!* Another Isadora Duncan!' gushed the guests. Leo basked in her success. Everybody kissed and cuddled the juvenile prodigy.

'She inherits it from me,' her mother smugly remarked. 'Poor Leo has no ear for harmony. His interests are purely antiquarian.' Overhearing her, he said: 'I suppose I count as an antique.' The one thing that grieved him as Lisa grew older was her dislike of picture galleries and of antiques in general. Hedy maliciously fostered this prejudice. 'Mamma tells me that your old junk is worth a fortune,' she said. 'What fun it will be to sell it when you are gone!' Leo blanched and said nothing but he took immediate precautions.

Whenever he added a new treasure to his collection Hedy insisted on his buying her a jewel or a fur coat of equivalent value. Since she complained of the discomfort of Renaissance furniture her boudoir was expensively redecorated in eighteenth-century style. There she held musical receptions from which Leo begged to be excused. 'You had better rest, you look tired,' she told him. 'Not tired, dear, bored', he answered.

'Who are all these people?' he asked on one of these occasions. 'Do I know anyone here? Do you? How on earth did you manage to rake them up? I hope there are no kleptomaniacs among them. They have a strange unwashed smell. We must fill the house with tuberoses.'

Hedy protested that her circle of music lovers was more distinguished than his crew of dilettanti, and most of them had titles as ancient as his bric-à-brac.

'Titled or not — and titles are commonplace here — they mustn't invade my privacy. They talk too loud. I can hear them from my study.'

'We want to start a society for the promotion of serious music. The Italians are not really musical. Puccini and Mascagni and that sort of stuff I don't call music. I'd exchange one Brahms quartet for the lot of them. As far as I can make out Florentines go to concerts to disturb them with coughs and gossip about their *nipotini*. They need to be educated. We must find them a first-class quartet . . .'

'But if they're not musical, as you maintain, you cannot force them to love Brahms.'

'They will, if they are given a chance to hear the best.'

The First World War intervened. Leo was almost as pro-German as his wife though he had never taken an interest in politics. For Hedy it was a question of 'my country right or wrong' and she had no doubt that the Kaiser was in the right; for Leo it was the superiority of German *Kultur*, his profound admiration for Wölfflin and Bode and other great scholars, which swayed his sentiments. But being an American citizen with an overriding loyalty to Harvard his German sympathy waned as the war continued, and when Hedy's parents were impoverished by the post-war inflation he viewed this as a personal vendetta.

The string quartet Hedy longed for turned up, as if from nowhere, in the aftermath of war. They were refugees from Riga, members of a single family, whom Leo had heard playing by chance in a picture restorer's studio. Instinctively he recognized their superlative quality and invited them to his tower. Hedy was overwhelmed by their performance. They

42

deserved to be better known. 'I never imagined you had so fine an ear,' she told Leo. They are *wunderbar* — extraordinary.' Her enthusiasm was unbounded and Leo caught fire from it.

A series of receptions were arranged for them and every audience, however mixed, agreed about their transcendental technique. Leo forgot his Leonardo horse for the time being. He provided them with new wardrobes, fed them and rebuilt his gardener's cottage for their dwelling. Finally he decided to become their impresario.

This was the modest beginning of the celebrated Solomon Quartet, which became a quintet when Hedy joined them. Through his influential relatives Leo launched them in New York, and from there they made a lightning tour of American cities. Hedy travelled with them and shared their hectic ovations. As their fame spread Leo retired to his tower at Arcetri, gladdened to be left alone.

Hedy had found a soul-satisfying occupation, together with four devoted retainers. But it was only with Isaac, the first violinist, that she formed a liaison. Physically he was so unprepossessing that Leo joked about it. 'I really think I am more personable but I suppose Isaac has a special charm of his own.' True, his features were transformed when he played his violin. His jet eyes flashed, his thick lips widened, he oozed an electric magnetism.

Lisa was finishing her education at a fashionable school in Switzerland which she described as absolute bliss. In Hedy's absence Leo's old cronies gathered round his paintings and portfolios and Van Becker, the doyen of restorers, was installed in the minstrels' gallery to clean his latest acquisition, a Tintoretto which Professor Bernichon attributed to El Greco — 'an early work by the Cretan master.' Students from Harvard and Yale came with letters of introduction and followed Leo up and down stairs from painting to sculpture, bewildered by his cascade of paradoxes. He treated the young with suave deference: 'Tell me what you feel about this? Would you accept it as the work of Spinello Aretino, or would you agree with Dr Offner that it is by Giovanni del Biondo? I should value your opinion.' With the old he was more diffident: 'So you've come to see the Leonardo horse? It is certainly a horse but the attribution is questionable. There are certain affinities, that is all one can say at present. As I grow older I find it more difficult to swallow the attributions of pedagogues. I'd sooner trust my cook. Let the object speak or sing to you. Listen to its unique message.'

Some pilgrims asked him: 'How does it feel to wake up with a masterpiece beside you every morning? I suppose you are so used to it that you cease to notice.'

'No, I notice something different every day. And sometimes I doubt my own vision and experience. In art as in nature there are so many bastards. The problems of authenticity begin to plague me. Perhaps a spiritual medium is required . . .'

'Quite like old times!' said Assunta. 'The Signore has become a bachelor again. Better that way!'

Often he stood silent while his visitors rhapsodized. He was stimulated by the variety of pilgrims to his tower.

Then a cablegram from Hedy summoned him to New York, where Isaac had been taken ill with acute bronchitis. The quartet had had to cancel their engagements and Leo's advice was urgently required.

Leo had not set foot in New York since introducing Hedy to his relatives soon after his marriage. He had been repelled by the bleakly perpendicular tokens of progress and he disliked the prospect of returning in mid-winter. Especially he disliked crossing the ocean. Being no sailor, ships gave him claustrophobia: he shied from contact with his fellow-passengers however genial, and they were usually too genial, inviting him to play poker or bridge, rattling dice and exchanging jokes at the bar, pacing the seesaw deck in boisterous weather. The compulsive optimism of his compatriots depressed him.

His *bête noire* Dr Hussander was also on board the steamer. He accosted Leo instantly: 'How's the Leonardo gee-gee? Have you altered his attribution?'

'Why not? It's half the fun of collecting.'

'Fun? For me it's just a matter of business. The art market depends on correct attributions. Consider the gulf between a Leonardo and a Boltraffio in hard cash. It makes me hate art, but I'm in it up to the neck. Caught in the quicksand!'

When Dr Hussander dogged him to the cabin where he had sought refuge Leo, forewarned by the fumes of his cigar, made terrible retching sounds to keep him out. He suffered more than usual on this voyage and tottered off the ship a partial wreck.

The prospect of seeing Hedy after his sabbatical season of quietude failed to soothe him. He had been so grateful to the quartet for taking her off that he dreaded the possible effect of Isaac's illness. Having launched the Solomon Quartet he felt under a moral obligation to support it. He had shaken himself free from Brooklyn long ago yet he had the sensation of returning to a school from which he had played truant. Fortunately there were many more private collections to be seen, apart from the museums enriched with fabulous bequests.

Escorted by three members of the quartet, Hedy met him at the dock with the news that Isaac was already out of danger. Though his temperature had fallen his spirits were very low. To cheer him up Hedy suggested that Leo should buy him a Stradivarius she had noticed at a sale of musical instruments. Whenever Hedy craved a particular object she became quite as tenacious as Leo and far more importunate. Albeit weakened by a chill he had caught on the voyage, he promised to gratify her. Anything for peace! The Stradivarius was duly purchased and presented to Isaac, whose excess of joy completed his recovery. Soon the Solomon Quartet were able to proceed on their tour of the Far West, leaving Leo in New York to recover from his chill. But in spite of a hacking cough he could not resist invitations to see the Widdrington, Flashman and Chute collections of Italian paintings. The houses were overheated by contrast with the freezing temperatures outside

45

them and, as if he were still in Florence, Leo often forgot his overcoat. His chill became feverish. A doctor diagnosed congestion of the lungs and consigned him to bed. Hedy was out of reach — not that her presence could have been therapeutic. Sienese saints and Madonnas flickered before his eyes in the hotel bedroom where a trained nurse hovered near him with potions to calm his delirium.

Leo stubbornly refused to be transported to hospital. 'Too late,' he muttered. Indeed, he was failing rapidly. He could only speak in stertorous whispers until he lapsed into a coma. The doctor shook his head. Before his relatives were summoned he had succumbed.

Playing to packed halls in Los Angeles, Hedy was unable to attend her husband's cremation. While her colleagues proceeded to South America she returned reluctantly to Florence where Lisa joined her. Mother and daughter had only themselves to blame for the provisions of Leo's will bequeathing the bulk of his collection to Florence and his Leonardo horse to Vinei. The considerable fortune he had left allowed Hedy to fill the gaps she now regretted. Yet Leo's Tower, deprived of its familiar masterpieces, was still redolent of his personality. Hedy began to realize that she missed him wherever she turned. She seemed to hear his languid drawl, his shuffling footsteps; a dull void replaced the atmosphere he had created. Ironically his mantle as collector had fallen on her and she began to haunt the antique shops, but the objects she bought were mediocre and she paid exorbitantly for them. Leo's former friends tried to influence her taste but she fancied she knew better. 'Poor Leo would turn in his grave if he could see what she is doing to his tower,' they said, oblivious that his ashes had been deposited in a Grecian urn.

Lisa had shot up into a winsome girl of seventeen precociously sophisticated and critical of her mamma, whose Americanisms, recently acquired, seemed incongruous. After a decent interval Hedy invited all Florence to a series of lavish At Homes, *thés dansants,* and cocktail parties, nominally for her daughter though she grabbed the few eligible bachelors to tango with cheek to cheek. Lisa despised ball-room dances: she preferred to invent dances of her own; and she was always willing to oblige by special request. She would pluck a flower from a vase and mime an intimate conversation with it, or capture an invisible bird on the wing and imitate its fluttering with her fingers, or hold a shell to her ear to listen to the murmur of the sea, swaying to the ebb and flow of the tide with glowing cheeks and quivering lips. Hedy was embarrassed by the sensuousness of her postures but her guests clamoured for them and shouted *Bis! Encore!*

When the Solomon Quartet returned from their transatlantic triumphs Isaac stepped into Leo's shoes, as it were. Success had turned him into a caricature of Don Juan. His Stradivarius had enhanced his reputation. While Lisa was still a child Hedy had no objection to his fondling of her, which she regarded partly as a tribute to herself, partly to his temperamental exuberance, but now that Lisa was full grown his lascivious pawings upset her. He accompanied Lisa's dancing on his violin, following her every movement with lustful eyes. 'She is an intensification of the joy of life,' he said, blowing her a kiss.

In fact Hedy was growing jealous — all the more since Isaac had cooled towards herself. He had been spoiled by American lion huntresses, she decided. He was neater, cleaner, more dapper than in his penurious days, but his features were quite as ugly. His batlike ears twitched between his heavy-lidded eyes and his lips were like overripe raspberries. And Hedy had once thought him beautiful! Now she shrank from his blubbery embraces. But when he drew his bow across the Stradivarius she saw him through a golden haze. He could evoke sensations of tropical heat and of Arctic cold, hallucinations of sunlight and moonlight. He had seldom played so magically as for Lisa. And when he stopped you could hear rose petals fall on the marble pavement in the hush before the thunder of applause.

Hedy had to admit that Isaac was now the chief magnet of

her salon, and she derived malicious pleasure from excluding those who had snubbed her in the past. But it galled her to think that her guests were attracted more by Isaac than by herself, and he behaved like a master of ceremonies. His air of condescension was intolerable when she remembered him as a half starved vagrant refugee. After all it was owing to her that he had a Stradivarius which had conferred the ultimate distinction on the Solomon Quartet, and since she had obtained it for him she considered it as a loan for which he was indebted to herself. He flourished the instrument with such a proprietary air that in spite of his virtuosity she winced with irritation. It seemed natural, however, that Isaac should replace Leo in Lisa's affections, but she failed to perceive that on Isaac's side the affection was more than paternal. His eagerness to play with and for Lisa amounted to an amorous pursuit whose ardour was strengthened by proximity. When she rehearsed her dances with him he would patiently repeat a complicated passage for her until she had perfected it. Hot and happy, she would reward him with a shower of kisses, of which he took greedy advantage. Opportunities to caress her were not lacking during Hedy's occasional absence and Lisa, full of gratitude, was susceptible to his transports of tenderness. She heard his violin while he embraced her. 'You are my inspiration,' he confided.

On her way to practise in the minstrels' gallery Hedy discovered the couple on a sofa in a compromising position. Lisa's under-bodice had been lowered and Isaac was nuzzling into her breasts. Hedy rushed up and slapped his face. '*Pfui*, you swine!' she shouted. 'I thought at least I could trust you with my daughter. And you even try to seduce her under my roof! Leave the house instantly. Never let me see your hideous mug again!'

'After all I'm her second father and might have been her first. Be reasonable, *liebchen!*'

'Shut your trap and leave this house!' She rang for the servants to remove his luggage.

'If he goes I go too,' Lisa protested.

'Run off to your bedroom and fasten your brassière, you ninny. Don't you realize he has been my lover?'

'Then you should forgive him for loving me also.'

'Never! To betray me with my own daughter under my eyes — that is unpardonable. He has behaved abominably.'

'But I want to marry him. He has proposed to me.'

'Don't be an idiot, he's old enough to be your father.'

'So was Daddy when he married you. That's the age I like best.'

'But there is a difference. What could Isaac offer you? The life of a wandering Bohemian. I won't hear of it. You'll never get my consent. Anyhow you are under age.'

Lisa wept and called her a tyrant but after a while she calmed down. Isaac had picked up his violin case and walked out with as much dignity as he could muster. He had not even glanced at Lisa or bidden her good-bye. Without music his fascination for Lisa evaporated. It had been a passing squall, exciting while it lasted.

The farewell concert of the Solomon Quartet in the Palazzo Vecchio — the Florentine town hall — was eminently a gala occasion. They played to a serried audience of vociferous enthusiasts: every seat had been reserved for double the usual price and the ladies were décolletées with glittering jewels. There were murmurs of disappointment when it was announced that the Schumann Quintet had been cancelled at the last moment 'owing to the pianist's indisposition.' The absence of Hedy was conspicuous, for her connection with the quartet was an open secret.

The applause was still echoing when there was a hubbub on the players' platform. Isaac was shouting and shaking his fist at a police officer who had arrived, belatedly, to confiscate his Stradivarius. There was a tussle before the instrument was removed, and Isaac was threatened with arrest for obstructing a public official in the course of his duty. The audience were informed that having been deprived of his instrument the first violinist was unable to continue. There was no alternative but to postpone the concert. Isaac sat weeping and wailing: 'My Stradivarius, my dearest possession! Now let me die!' The scene aroused mass indignation and sympathy for the persecuted artist. In the meantime a distinguished member of the audience volunteered to lend Isaac his own violin, a priceless Amati. Though prostrated by the loss of his own instrument Isaac rose to thank him. After a considerable delay the quartet was able to continue, encouraged by renewed acclamations from the frustrated public. The quartet snatched victory from the jaws of defeat, for Isaac surpassed himself in virtuosity.

The dramatic interruption had been a challenge but it had also been a strain. He broke down after the concert, which was extolled by the leading musical critics. But they could not console him for his bereavement.

'I have been castrated,' he wailed.

When the details were published Hedy was universally blamed, but she had had her revenge. Having kept the bill of sale and paid for its annual insurance, she could prove that the Stradivarius was hers. She had decided to sell Leo's Tower with most of its contents and take Lisa to New York. Leo's prophecy about the fate of private art collections was thus fulfilled in his particular case. His cherished paintings and sculpture had already been dispersed: now his residence was to be transformed into a cosmetic surgery clinic. Only a few art historians could trace the whereabouts of his legacy to Florence: three small predellas (ascribed to Beccafumi) were stolen, apparently by acrobats, and have not been recovered yet. The famous bronze horse, no longer attributed to Leonardo, was relegated to the natural history museum.

The Solomon Quartet were also dispersed, and only gramophone records give ghostly renderings of their performances. Isaac was last heard of playing Hungarian *czardas* in a Parisian night-club. His colleagues were reduced to playing popular melodies in hotel dining rooms. The

Stradivarius lies silent in the bowels of a Brooklyn bank.

Hedy settled in Hollywood, where her daughter married a prominent film producer. As co-founder of an academy for the development of spiritual expression she is a local celebrity. When she speaks of Leo, always with reverence, her voice and accents are uncannily reminiscent of his own. Her account of the Leonardo horse and its discovery is a saga which her son-in-law hopes to produce as a film in the style of Buñuel. But she has no nostalgia for Florence. Despising figurative art as too materialistic, she has become a proselyte and practitioner of pure abstraction. Her straight lines, crossed lines and circles compete with the mystical associations of blankness, and her collection of pieces of driftwood from Californian beaches is perhaps unique.

Saint Gabriel

Certain bipeds seem to have been born for the sole purpose of entertaining mankind. Gabriel Disher had this special vocation, for which he enjoyed an ephemeral fame in Paris between the two World Wars. He was the social impresario of lavish parties for which others were glad to pay. By a fashionable cosmopolitan coterie he was considered an arbiter of taste though he possessed more flair than culture. The so-called jet-setters are the modern equivalents of that coterie. Having survived the holocaust of the First World War they had grown indifferent to politics and contemptuous of politicians. They stopped their ears to the rumours of approaching hostilities and made as much hay as they could while the sun was shining. And the sun shone brightly, cynically, while they capered among the haycocks.

Those were the days, or nights, of extravagant festivities, usually in fancy dress, and Gabriel was invariably consulted about their preparation. He organised parties in the Bois de Boulogne, on barges on the Seine, at Saint-Germain and Fontainebleau and, perhaps the most memorable, on the Eiffel Tower, nominally to celebrate its inauguration in 1889. This had involved much strenuous wire-pulling and greasing of palms. The police were out in full force to protect the guests from proletarian rowdies but the mob of onlookers at the foot of the tower applauded the impromptu pageant with boisterous enthusiasm. Every type of conveyance from De Dion-Bouton motors to tandem bicycles and dog-carts drove up with the guests in exaggerated costumes of the period. Preposterous hats, feather boas and muffs prevailed among the women; flowing whiskers and garish uniforms of many nationalities among the men, who danced frantically to the strains of a Hungerian orchestra above the roofs of the flickering Ville Lumière.

As master of the revels Gabriel took his rôle seriously, but in every other respect he was frivolous. Except that he was English little was known about his origin. At the age of twenty-five he had come to Paris as private secretary to Baron Theophile de Lornier, the plutocratic art collector, but his job was an ornamental sinecure. The Baron, an ardent Anglophile, was kept in touch with England, as it were, by his handsome young secretary. Gabriel also acted as unofficial tutor to the Baron's children and a sort of *cicisbeo* to Sabine, his mettlesome little wife. After a Parisian residence of over a decade Gabriel remained English in appearance, voice and accent yet he had adapted himself perfectly to the Lorniers' style of life and their friends regarded him as a member of the family. Though their relationship was platonic the Baroness doted on him: she never bought a dress or a hat without his approval. 'Gab knows what suits me better than I do myself,' she said.

For the children, three daughters and a son, he was an enterprising playmate, teaching them tennis, golf, and innocent indoor games. But children are ungrateful, and when they grew up they treated him as a superannuated schoolboy. Aristide, the son, looked down on him as insufficiently manly while taking advantage of his good nature: Gab was always so obliging. Indeed, he felt more at ease with women than with men, the Baron excepted. Gab was the privileged household pet, the confidant and counsellor of both husband and wife. When any difficulty arose, it was 'Let's ask dear Gab!' Cool and collected yet never conspicuous, he supervised their luncheons and dinners and arranged the *placements* — who was to sit next to whom. Apart from a few flippant interjections he let others do the talking and, my word, how they talked! His little half-smile stimulated spicy gossip.

Gab could be disarmingly personal in an offhand manner.

'Are those the pearls I gave you, Suzy? I'd forgotten I broke the bank at Monte Carlo . . .' 'My dear, that hat! Why not wear a stuffed seagull while you're about it?' But though this could verge on impertinence the ladies never took offence, for unlike most men of their acquaintance he had the virtue of noticing every detail of their *toilette* and he remembered what they had worn at a previous meeting. It was always some titled woman who called him to the telephone, and he answered in a brisk matter-of-fact voice. 'Come, come, let's be democratic, dear Duchess. Let's begin at the Boeuf and end in the rue de Lappe. I'm in the mood for a spree. Don't scold me if I get squiffy.'

He was a regular client of the *Boeuf sur le Toit*, where after a few drinks he was apt to wriggle and pull funny faces, repeating the old refrain (which flummoxed them), 'Hinky pinky parley voo.' *'Tu es impayable,'* shrilled the Duchess de Souchy. *'Mais je te ferai payer, chérie,'* he retorted, licking his lips, 'Come along, let's boogie-woogie. It's one of my favourite tunes.' And off they swept between the jigging dancers, palm to palm towards the hypnotic saxophone.

The boys at the bar couldn't take their eyes off Gab, the only male in a bevy of chic matrons. Later on he would offer them drinks and exchange light banter with them. They did not object to his calling them froggies — *'mes copains les grenouilles'*. 'He's really one of us,' they said, 'but he finds the dames more profitable. Have you noticed his Cartier bracelet and the watch on each wrist? It takes an Englishman to be that eccentric.' He was caricatured as *'Rosbif anglais au Boeuf parisien'*, a *rosbif* that was certainly not *saignant;* and Cocteau drew several calligraphic versions of his profile.

Had it not been for Gabriel, the Baron and Baroness de Lornier might have drifted apart. When they quarrelled over the exorbitant purchase of a medieval reliquary casket instead of a Nattier the Baroness coveted, it was Gab's debonair diplomacy that drew them together and the Nattier was procured as a peace offering. Theirs had been a successful *mariage de convenance* to consolidate two great Franco-Belgian

54

fortunes, cemented by mutual tolerance, consanguinity partly Jewish, and infatuation for Gab. Their town mansion, the Villa Pompeienne on the avenue des Champs-Elysées, contained a priceless medley of Christian and pagan artefacts which had no appeal for the Baroness. She described it as a beautiful background for boring conversations, bored stiff, as she said, by the critics and art dealers who monopolised the Baron and swept him off to sales at a moment's notice. His collection of crucifixes made her uncomfortable and his paintings repelled her. 'Do you want to drive me to hysterics?' she told him when he proudly produced an expensive nightmare by Goya. One of their worst scenes was caused by the rearrangement of her boudoir while the Baron was in New York. Having banished all the Renoirs and the furniture by Boulle and Riesener, she had turned it into a combination of conservatory and aquarium with glass tanks of shimmering fish built into the walls. Gab had selected the plants, which were as varied as the striped and speckled fish darting among the tendrils of live coral or floating beside a frilly sea anemone. 'All so much more alive than your lobster-women by Renoir,' she remarked, when the Baron returned with another lobster-hued bather by that plethoric painter. All Gab's tact had been required to soothe the Baron's anger.

Without any parental pose, and perhaps on that account, the Baron had endeared himself to his children, who were fonder of him than of their too maternal mamma. Sabine had fussed over her daughters with excessive solicitude until they married and settled down with suitable husbands in London, Rome and Brussels, after which she lost interest in them. Aristide as an anaemic child had demanded all her care, thanks to which he had grown robust and inordinately conceited, a priggish Mr Know-all. Though she never admitted it Sabine was disappointed in her offspring and allowed her husband to spoil them to his heart's content. She was aware that they sneered at Gab, who had done more than Theo to brighten their childhood. They showed their resentment of his position in the household in many little ways which did not escape her observation. Aristide spoke of his 'Eminence rose' and nicknamed him *'La demoiselle élue.'*

But Gab's position was impregnable, and when the Baron died suddenly of a blood-clot Sabine decided that she could not live without him. To the family's embarrassment and indignation she married the Baron's former secretary. 'Your father would have wished it,' she told her children, and they could do nothing to prevent the marriage. Sabine was fifty-five, and Gab about forty, so well preserved that one could not guess their ages.

As Mrs Gabriel Disher Sabine became a British subject. Aristide inherited the Villa Pompeienne and its fabulous treasures, becoming (in Walt Whitman's phrase) 'demented with the mania of owning things', even more so than his father had been. Sabine and Gab went to England, where everybody and everything delighted her, including the simpler cuisine. 'I feel I'm on solid ground among solid people,' she declared. 'I've begun a new life. *Je raffole de* steak and kidney pie.'

Most extraordinary for a lapsed Catholic she became infatuated with the Anglican Church. The services in Westminster Abbey moved her to tears. Although she could not join the singing the hymns were a powerful attraction, for they reminded her of her childhood when her English governess warbled them to her at bed time. Though Gab was immune to this access of piety he felt obliged to accompany her to services which bored him so that he fortified himself with double Martinis in advance. Furtively he fortified himself more and more. As a married man he had to sacrifice his noctambulous habits: in London he could find no substitute for the *Boeuf sur le Toit*. Without the exhilarating ping-pong of Parisian persiflage he began to feel out of his element. He pored over French newspapers and magazines with acute nostalgia while waiting to escort Sabine to Harrods or some other emporium. Her energy for shopping expeditions exhausted him, for as usual she bought no garment without his approval.

While she was relieved to have cast off her domestic trammels, Gab hankered after the amenities of Paris. The theatre was his chief resource and compensation. He never wearied of Noël Coward and knew his lyrics by heart: his clipped accent and nonchalant tone were uncannily like the versatile Master's. *Parisian Pierrot,* that's me,' he used to say airily. 'And *A Room with a View* must have been composed for us,' said Sabine, who discerned a surprising affinity between them. Perhaps it was the song *Mad Dogs and Englishmen* which prompted Gab with a desire to travel. 'Let's move on for a honeymoon in the sun,' he suggested. 'I should like a taste of the tropics for a change. Don't you think it would freshen us up to go on a lovely cruise, see other countries, birds and beasts and flowers? What about it, old girl?'

'*Pourquoi pas? D'accord. L'embarquement pour Cythère* . . . I leave the arrangements to you. You do look as if you need a tonic.'

The honeymoon was deliciously prolonged. They were still in the Pacific while the war-clouds were gathering over Europe. Gab, ever matey and gregarious, struck up new friendships on sea and land, especially in the bar-rooms. They were in Canada when the Second World War broke out, and the hospitable Canadians persuaded them to linger there.

Aristide having fled to North Africa was able to correspond with them after the fall of Paris, which affected Gab more intensely than Sabine. Both of them remained optimistic in spite of the disastrous news. Sabine cherished a mystical faith in Winston Churchill, while Gab was an ardent supporter of General de Gaulle.

Gab longed to return to Paris after the liberation but Sabine was more in favour of London. They compromised over Florence, where both had a variety of artistic friends. On the way they stopped in Paris, but Sabine refused to stay with Aristide at the Villa Pompeienne, memories of which disquieted her. Thanks to her son-in-law in the Spanish embassy the house with all its treasures had been protected.

During their family reunion Aristide had been so

patronizing to Gab that Sabine was deeply offended. 'My sisters and I feel indebted to you for looking after Mamma,' he told him. 'It was a great comfort to know that she was safe in Canada while I was roughing it in Algiers and Dakar. I suppose the winters were chilly, but at least the houses were heated and there was enough grub to nourish you. And I hope you found some congenial night spots in Winnipeg, or was it Quebec? Not too dismal a war. Well, I'm sorry you would not accept my hospitality. What made you choose such a backwater as Florence — a sunny place for shady people, eh?'

'Don't be so bloody supercilious,' said Gab. 'We couldn't all be war heroes, you know. You were jolly lucky to slip away before the occupation and come back to find your home in mint condition.'

'It was because I never stopped praying for you,' said Sabine.

'Since when have you taken up religion, Mamma?'

'Ever since you were born.'

'Funny that I never noticed it.'

'My religion is purely personal. It is not a subject I'm prepared to discuss at present. Anyhow, I don't like your tone. Remember I'm your mother. It is time you got married. A good wife would mend your manners.'

'Let him sow his wild oats first,' said Gab to mollify her.

'He has sown enough already. I hope you have a clean bill of health since your return from Africa.'

They parted on frigid terms. 'Aristide was always a prig,' she remarked. 'Being an only son the Baron spoiled him.'

In Florence Sabine soon found an ideal villa at Bellosguardo with a glorious panorama of the city. The green expanse sloping down to a vineyard was its main attraction for Gab. White pigeons fluttered in and out of the open windows and the place was in a pitiable state of neglect before they took possession, but Gab was fired with the ambition to convert the grounds into an orderly English garden — no statues, no fountains, none of that pompous claptrap. So he immediately set about planting the flowers he preferred in herbaceous borders divided by a gravel walk and a stretch of grass lawn in which oblong beds were cut, leading to a bower of lilac bushes. The back of the house was covered with roses and jasmine; the front courtyard was filled with white azaleas in pots. The interior was enlarged by the removal of several partitions and the introduction of plate-glass windows for the living room, facing a view of the valley towards Fiesole and Monte Morello.

Gab discovered new resources as a gardener and became immersed in botanical literature, while Sabine studied the trend of the stock market and made investments by telephone to the Bourse, for she had inherited a flair for financial transactions.

Their society was confined to a few old cronies at teatime. Both revelled in the informality of their Florentine existence.

When summoned to the telephone Gab was usually to be found pruning the roses in his shirt-sleeves, pulling up weeds, or battling with brambles in the shrubbery. He never learned Italian, but his assistants became accustomed to his individual Esperanto, a farcical farrago of English, French, and 'the lingo', accompanied by appropriate gestures. 'Venez ici pronto . . . mette più acqua . . . donnez-moi (pointing to his chest) spada . . . soyez gentile con le rose . . . bisogna manure, caca . . . That's the stuff! We're getting on splendido. Bravo!'

The garden resounded with laughter and bursts of song. 'I'm picking up a lot of their lingo,' he said. 'Better than any Berlitz school.'

Now and then he wandered to the stanzone, or lemon house, where he hoarded a supply of booze undetected by Sabine, who kept a censorious eye on his consumption of strong waters. In fact he drank more than was good for him, though this was only betrayed by a dreamy vagueness and a tendency to titter for no apparent reason. Instead of the glamorous parties he used to organize in Paris he was organizing colour schemes for his herbaceous borders, and Sabine basked in the botanical paradise he was creating. As the only genuine English garden near Florence it became famous: on specific days it was open to the public by special request. The tourists provided Gab with gratuitous diversion, some of them handed him a tip of five hundred *lire*. To those who tried to pick his gardenias he had to speak severely. How astonished they were when he scolded them in English!

Inevitably Parisian friends turned up whom neither had seen since the war. 'We miss you sadly,' they told Gab. 'None of the parties are such fun as when you were with us. No originality. Charlie only entertains in his Venetian palazzo — all very grand but he lacks *entrain,* besides he is far too snobbish. Arturo does things in more theatrical style but he's obsessed with Louis XIV. Since he couldn't get permission to rent Versailles for his birthday he has been out of sorts. There has been nothing to compare with your gala at the Eiffel Tower. Democracy is becoming puritanical. We need you to shake us up. Don't you find Florence absurdly provincial? After seeing the sights what on earth is there to do?'

'The garden keeps me fully occupied. Don't you think it is worth it?'

Sabine maintained that she had never been so happy, for she had Gab all to herself. Her eyes rested on him fondly while he snipped off the dead heads with his secateurs or flourished his watering can. Clad in a turquoise-blue boiler suit with yellow leather gauntlets, he looked every inch a gardener in a musical comedy. The only thing that worried her was his tippling. Sometimes he lost his balance and his speech became blurred. Though she pretended not to notice she ordered the butler to hide the gin and whisky, and she removed several bottles from his dressing-room. Gardening should have given him an appetite but he merely pecked at his food when Sabine had taken trouble with the menu. 'You eat my dinner, dear. What I need is a drink,' he said.

'You seem to have had one too many.'

He bent over to kiss her hand, smothering a hiccup. 'After all day in the garden I really deserve one,' he pleaded.

'Well, just for this once,' she sighed. 'But it isn't good for you, you know.'

There were moments when she was almost jealous of the garden, for she had not discovered his cache in the lemon house. She tried in vain to inveigle him into the Anglican Church on Via Maggio whose jovial chaplain was one of their most assiduous guests. Though shy of her clerical clique Gab made an exception for Archdeacon Stubble, who reminded him of his favourite comedian George Robey. 'I wish you'd pop into my church on Sundays — for your own sake as well as mine. Sabine must have told you how snug and cosy it is. If you choose the text I'll preach a special sermon for your benefit. I don't mind saying that I'm a champion preacher!'

'Sorry, padre, I can't trust myself not to giggle. My church is the garden. I'm pretty sure God walks there as in the poem, "A garden is a lovesome thing, God wot", fern grot, rose plot — I forget how it goes. Not that I'm the least bit pi but I get a feeling of uplift too difficult to explain.'

'To have roses in our garden we must have roses in our heart. I suspect Gab is really a mystic,' the Archdeacon told Sabine.

'I'm sure you're right,' she agreed.

Sabine's Italian was hardly more fluent than Gab's, yet she managed to chat quite volubly with Don Fabrizio, the parish priest, when he came to bless the villa, room by room. He too had hinted at Gab's spirituality. 'He has the face of a Donatello saint,' he declared. How true, she reflected. He had saved her from an existence of crass materialism; he had helped her by his joy, the grace men say to God. She began to find hidden meanings in his casual utterances. Now what did he mean by... He kept her guessing.

Though he seemed to bear the bonds of marriage lightly Gab began to show signs of strain by a nervous twitch. 'I've come to the conclusion that I'm not domestic,' he confided to me when I met him in front of Doney's. 'You're lucky to be a bachelor free as air.'

'Nobody is free as air, Gab, that's an illusion.'

61

'Well, you can have a drink whenever you want one. I can't. *Verboten.* The wife won't let me. Let's have one now while she's nattering with the Archdeacon. What's yours? A double whisky for me, presto. Call that a proper double? Hey, hand me the bottle . . . As I was saying, mind you don't marry. It's a kind of hell.'

'You shock me: this is blasphemy. Blest with so devoted a wife . . .'

'Too devoted. A millstone round my neck. If I've taken to the bottle you'll know why. Mum's the word: I've only myself to blame. Remember the old song: "You made me love you. I didn't want to do it, I didn't want to do it." That's me all over. Too late to mend. I love the old girl. It's a kind of hell all the same. I've become a smuggler, sneaking in with hooch through the back door. Do I look blotto? Never mind: another of the same. *Doppio doppio.* That's more like it . . .' He chuckled. 'Could you spare me a gasper? That's also *verboten,* have to creep into the loo to light up . . . Forgive me for letting off steam: I'm at the end of my tether. Hell's bells, here comes the family bus with the missus. You must help me to invent an alibi.'

While Sabine sat inside the Rolls beside the Archdeacon the chauffeur called for Signor Gabriele in the bar. 'Am I still presentable? I'll have to watch my step,' he muttered. 'Come and say hullo to Sabine.' He braced himself with effort. Considering that he spent so much time in the pure air of Bellosguardo he looked far from well. His features were drawn and wrinkled despite his artificial suntan.

Absorbed in an argument about the Trinity with the Archdeacon, whose explanation perplexed her, Sabine failed to notice Gab's condition, but the Archdeacon observed that he looked 'a bit off colour.' In fact he felt so unwell that he had to lie down. 'Just a passing malaise,' he murmured, 'I'll soon be all right.' Sabine was to treasure these words as a profound comment on the human predicament.

Eventually a doctor was called against Gab's wish, but he came too late to do more than pronounce a mistaken diagnosis, prescribing a modicum of brandy on the kill-or-cure principle. Soon Gab fell into a coma from which he rallied at intervals to gulp a drop of brandy and croon snatches of the songs he had sung in his heyday. 'I can't give you anything but love, baby' alternated with 'Ten cents a dance' and 'Hard-hearted Hannah, the vamp of Savannah' when Sabine, or the nurse on duty, refused to pour him an extra dose. While Sabine, struggling with her tears, suggested 'Lead, Kindly Light' Gab said audibly: 'Keep up your pecker, old girl, I've not cooled yet.'

Not long before his final coma Gab quavered, 'Nothing but blue skies from now on.' He died with a seraphic smile. Sabine was convinced that his bedroom was filled with a sky-blue vapour and that she heard the fluttering of an angel's wings. Henceforth it became the sanctuary where she went to meditate. Except the empty bottles and medicine tray everything remained *in situ* as Gab had left it: his presence still hovered near her. This presence gained spiritual intensity: it was as if Sabine had passed through the valley of the shadow and come out into dazzling sunlight. Her fears and anxieties evaporated with Gab's dissolution. Gab spoke to her not only indoors but outside in the garden, from the herbaceous borders and a corner of the *stanzone* where an anachronistic cocktail shaker was discovered.

Sabine felt guided, protected, uplifted as never before, and she looked several years younger. Since Gab had made her promise not to wear mourning her clerical friends were shocked by the brilliance of her attire, consisting, as she told them, of the dresses he had chosen. They could not help goggling, when she described the hours of meditation, or communion with his spirit, as 'entering the silence', for apparently Gab had a lot to communicate about every conceivable topic ranging from North Ireland to South Africa. For Sabine he was more truly alive than when he was on this earth and she was visibly serene in consequence.

Every day fresh flowers from the sanctified garden filled the

Venetian vase in front of his enlarged photograph framed in massive silver. The photograph was a good likeness of Gabriel standing in a characteristically careless pose, smiling that half smile which had endeared him to so many of his friends. To those who had known him in his Parisian prime the smile seemed faintly ironical, for he had never pretended to be pious and now he was spoken of as a full-blooded saint awaiting canonization. Every night he revealed to Sabine what was going to happen in the world below, and the morning newspapers would confirm it. If the Press chanced to contradict him, they would corroborate his statements on the morrow.

Armed with advance information from so incontestable a source Sabine replied to the sceptical with a single decisive gesture: the index finger of her right hand would point towards the ceiling and beyond it to the heaven above. It was impossible to contradict her, for she knew. This absolute certainty gave her sweetness and strength. Since Gab's passing she had beatified him.

The old cronies who came to pay her their respects — not to mention the members of her family — were flabbergasted by this transmogrification, so remote from their recollections of Gab in the flesh. For all his spontaneous acts of kindness and altruism nobody could have suspected that he was ripe for canonization. A man-about-town full of jokes and light gossip, he had never suggested a dual personality. But after listening to Sabine they began to doubt the reality of their impressions. What if he had been a holy man in secret, spending the day in penitence after a night on the tiles? At Montmartre in the early hours, come to think of it, his features had had an ascetic *je ne sais quoi* . . . Sabine almost convinced one. Then one glanced at his photograph, so dapper in a grey flannel suit, the conventional carnation in his buttonhole, the air of faint mockery, and one concluded, no: if this was a saint, he was a saint of the mundane; Sabine had been mundane when she married him.

Even Gab would have been astonished at all the charities linked to his name, the commemorative chapel in the garden, the local church entirely restored, the car park with public lavatories beside it, the football field, the school for handicapped children. Gab's name was an Open Sesame to Sabine's capacious purse. From the distance her scattered relations observed this reckless expenditure with alarm and disapproval. When they came to visit her at Christmas and Easter they were obliged to reserve rooms in a hotel lest their presence in the house interrupted the current of her subliminal intercourse. She became increasingly detached from the members of her family, who could not share her philanthropic fervour. As she grew older she let them understand that they tired her. 'We live on different planes,' she said. 'They do not need me and I do not need them.'

Her vintage Rolls Royce was too big and broad for the Florentine highways and byways, so she sold it at a loss and handed the proceeds to Don Fabrizio. The family bus, as Gab called it, was equipped with a backgammon set and a table for card-games, which were presented to the priest as venerable mementoes.

It was Don Fabrizio who had proposed the inauguration of a football field since Gab had fraternized with the footballers in his parish. Sabine agreed that it would be an opportune tribute to his memory. When the field was ready Sabine issued invitations for the opening ceremony. It was a pity that none of her grandchildren were able to attend it, for the Communist mayor delivered an eloquent panegyric upon the English comrade who had set so splendid an example of athletic democracy. 'Well was he christened Gabriel, an angel among the angels!' said Don Fabrizio, who had organized a procession of young footballers with a local band playing the march from *Alda* with more vigour than harmony. The goals were adorned with Anglo-Italian flags; the field was blessed with unction; and the first ball was kicked off to a salvo of applause. *Evviva Don Gabriele!* It was all very noisy, an explosion of youthful energy.

65

Sabine was not interested in the game *per se,* but she felt certain that Gab was also blessing the occasion. The site of the field had been chosen by Don Fabrizio on behalf of Gab, who had spoken to him in a dream. He was actually wearing a halo . . . 'A spiritual football field,' he said. 'It will keep the dear boys out of mischief.' Sabine invited him with the mayor to a substantial meal of which she could not partake as she always ate alone since her widowhood, but she could enjoy their gastronomic gusto and appreciative belching. If only she could understand what they were saying, for the more they ate the louder their voices boomed. The mayor had raised a topic anathema to the priest — that of abortion. How very delightful Italians were, she mused, they made conversation excitingly dramatic. These nearly came to blows: at one moment fists were flourished. But they parted amicably after their altercation and the mayor promised to forbid abortion in his own family.

Sabine's weekly At Homes to her clerical friends and their appendages were strictly ecumenical. Don Fabrizio was the first to arrive and the last to leave. Archdeacon Stubble and the Reverend Lincoln Blotch, pastor of the Episcopalian congregation, rubbed shoulders with a bevy of Irish and American nuns. Tables were piled with succulent sandwiches, chocolate and plum cakes, eclairs and meringues bursting with whipped cream, and Sabine saw that the dishes were constantly replenished. Kentucky Bourbon was provided for the American pastor, *vin santo* for Don Fabrizio, Bristol Milk for Archdeacon Stubble. After the repast Sabine conducted her guests to the chapel for a prayer of thanksgiving and a communal hymn. All of them agreed with her that the place had an aura of peculiar sanctity. A rumour that she intended to leave her property to the Church enhanced the assiduity of her regular visitors. Which Church? was the question debated among the rivals, who were not averse from sectarian intrigue. But as the American pastor was wont to proclaim, 'The unexpected is the Kentucky Bourbon of life.'

At the age of ninety, in spite of the most sophisticated

hearing aids, Sabine's deafness precluded verbal intercourse with mortals except within closest range. But she could hear the voice of Gab from above quite distinctly, and he continued to tell her far more than any newspaper about cosmic happenings. There were certain cryptic allusions which defied elucidation, such as 'Begin the biguine', referring to Israel, and 'Ban, Ban, Cacaliban', referring to Prime Minister Callaghan. Even in ethereal spirit Gab had not lost his puckish sense of humour.

Fin de Race

'An attractive young American couple in love with Florence and looking for an old villa — I've asked them in for tea.'

'Oh dear, most of our Crown Derby's chipped — Giulio's too vain to wear spectacles. I'll have to borrow some decent cups from the Cuthbertsons. Do call at Doney's for some cakes on your way home, crispy for you and creamy for me. The seed cake's mouldy.'

'Righto, old girl.' Terence pecked his adoring spouse on the cheek. 'You might furbish up the guest-rooms just in case . . .'

The Sperrys' villa was really too big for them and their expenses had been mounting since the drains had been overhauled and the whole front had been replastered: more bills kept rolling in and they were feeling the pinch. If they could let their upper floor, it would be a bonus. The only fly in the ointment was Terence's susceptibility to skirts. Priscilla was sadly conscious of her plainness but she could rely on her Irish vivacity as a compensation. Terence, who had been handicapped by partial paralysis, depended on her moral and physical support. He drove his gig to the office, and she helped him to climb into it. His broad grin as he waved au revoir warmed the cockles of her heart. She tripped into the house to get everything ship-shape.

When the young couple drove up in a carriage Priscilla rushed out to welcome them. 'Hello, my dears!' she shrilled, seizing the little wife with both arms and pulling her out of the cab. 'Terence never told me that you are a gloire de Dijon rose, he was afraid I might be jealous. But you *are* a perfect rose and no mistake. May I kiss you?'

Bella Overton found herself enveloped in a bosomy embrace

while Terence mumbled an introduction to Mr and Mrs Overton of Boston. 'Mr Overton is an architect,' he explained. 'He wants a Cinquecento villa like ours but he hasn't found one yet. I've promised to investigate. Step inside. You'll need a dish of tea after your excursion.'

'The drive up the hill was divine,' said Bella. 'So many gardens with high gates and crumbling walls, and cypresses and olives. I longed to know who owned them, what romantic lives they must lead.'

'You'll soon find out, if you're not in a hurry. This is a very sociable neighbourhood.'

Priscilla conducted them through a spacious hall into a high-ceilinged drawing-room cluttered with ancient bric-à-brac. She poured tea at a table piled with pyramids of assorted cakes.

'What delicious tea, Mrs Sperry.'

'I get it from my brother in Ceylon. He's a tea-planter out there.'

'How splendid. We should all plant something in this life but so few of us do. When we find our Tuscan villa I hope to plant hundreds of flowers. Do you cultivate a garden, Mrs Sperry?'

'Ours is just a glorified orchard with lemons in pots. Do call me Priscilla, dear, and what may I call you? Why stand on ceremony? Bless you for coming. You're a sight for sore eyes.'

'Everybody calls me Bella, short for Arabella.'

'Bella meaning beautiful. It fits you like a glove.'

While the women prattled Terence expatiated on a Della Robbia figure he had picked up 'for a song', a suave Saint Sebastian without arrows, and showed Overton some other treasures.

'Don't leave little me out of it,' exclaimed Bella. 'I'm crazy for antiques. Show us everything! Take us all over the house from top to bottom.'

Overton particularly admired the carved oak beams of the ceiling and the *pietra serena* chimney-piece.

'We have piggies to heat the bedrooms — that's what we call

our portable stoves — they give out a wonderful warmth. And charcoal braziers to warm our beds in winter — the Italians call them "priests" — picturesque as well as practical. Now follow me, dears.'

They climbed a balustraded staircase and Priscilla led them through a red-tiled corridor to the upper chambers. They were capacious but sparsely furnished. Priscilla assured them that the beds were more comfy than they looked. 'I made a bloomer when I ordered that four-poster. I asked for a *letto a quattro posti*. "A bed for four persons, Signora?" You should have seen the carpenter's face!'

The baths were marble sarcophagi which the maid had to fill from buckets of hot water.

'It must seem very primitive to you Americans. We live as in the Cinquecento without electricity, only candles and oil-lamps. Actually we prefer them, so much cosier!'

The candles flickering in strategic positions against strips of blue velvet and crimson brocade diffused a mystical aura. 'It's blissfully restful,' said Bella. 'The most friendly and sympathetic villa we've seen. Could you help us to find a place like it?'

'So our cottage has caught your fancy? It was practically a shell when we moved in to it. All you behold is my Terence's creation. He furnished it bit by bit with loving care. But times have changed: we couldn't afford that now.'

'I suppose,' said Overton boldly, 'you wouldn't consider letting it to us?'

Terence pondered with an awkward smile and scratched his head. 'But what would Priscilla and I do in the meantime? And what would you dear people do with us?'

'Couldn't we persuade you to stay on? Surely the house is roomy enough for the four of us. Oh please say yes!' Bella pleaded.

Priscilla hugged her effusively and turned to Terence. 'Wouldn't it be fun to give it a trial?' she coaxed him.

'Be a good sport!' Bella added. 'Let's risk the experiment. I simply adore this place: it was love at first sight. So does Felix, but he's a man of few words.'

'No harm in trying,' said Terence. 'To anyone else I'd say no, but I'm bowled over by your honest enthusiasm. For once Priscilla's not exaggerating. I've put the best part of myself into every nook and cranny of this villa.'

So, barely a week after their arrival in Florence, Felix and Bella Overton settled with a cartload of Vuitton trunks in the Villa Sperry at Arcetri. The rent was higher than they had anticipated, but it included the owners, their domestic staff, and their prolonged experience of Tuscan ways and means free of extra charge.

The Sperrys were intensely sociable. Their Saturday At Homes were packed with a cosmopolitan crowd of expatriates, part conventional, part bohemian, whose private histories, fads and foibles, were recounted by Priscilla with exhuberant relish. Most of them appeared to dislike each other, especially the art historians. Of the latter it was hard to ascertain who was on speaking terms from one day to the next. Between the buttered toast and the teapot the air was dense with intrigue. 'The vibrations are as visible as cigar smoke,' said Naomi Pratt who went in for spiritualism.

Felix was too busy reconnoitring the countryside to participate unless he encountered a fellow architect. Bella lolled on a sofa observing the guests with a lazy smile. She was the passive recipient of much unsolicited advice as to whom and what she should avoid, but her lack of response was discouraging. The others belonged to an older generation: they were more amusing to hear about than to meet and she could not be bothered with small talk. She seemed to be waiting for a stage curtain to rise.

'Darling, are you bored?' Priscilla asked her. 'I've collected all Florence to meet you — I mean the Florence that matters. They'll invite you to their country estates and their art collections, if you give them a chance, but you'll scare them away if you remain so aloof.'

'Don't worry. I'm quite happy gathering impressions.'

'I hope they are pleasant ones. I was afraid you were feeling lonesome without Felix. I presume he is house-hunting. We dread the day when you pack those heavy trunks.'

'That's a long way off. Felix is a perfectionist like me. Situation, proportions, dimensions — the villa must be just right. Perhaps he'll end by building one from scratch.'

When the guests departed Priscilla relaxed to discuss them over a glass of vermouth. 'Poor Theodosia. You'd never believe she was once a *femme fatale*. Her career till the age of fifty was littered with broken hearts. Her first husband was killed in a duel, her second in a toboggan: they say she brings bad luck. Now she goes in for gigolos: that's why she's had to give up Monte-Carlo . . .' and so forth.

'Do tell me,' Bella interjected, 'who was the fat marchesa in widow's weeds with a Boston accent? She raved about her brilliant son, insisted that we ought to meet. Somehow I didn't take to her though she couldn't have been more affable. There's something vaguely sinister about her.'

'Oh, the Marchesa Buondelmonte. She was born near Boston but brought up in Florence and married into one of the oldest families, now sadly impoverished. Her son, Aldo, is certainly a stunner, but he is not a lady's man. He got into a nasty scrape: Felix would not approve. Terence and I keep in touch with him for his mother's sake though he is socially taboo.'

'He sounds intriguing. Was it a financial scrape? That's pardonable if he's poor.'

'I'm afraid it's a matter of morals. He was forced to leave his regiment on account of a scandal. There are plenty of fairies about but they try to hide it. That's the one thing frowned upon by Florentine society.'

'Why should anyone care? Maybe he never met the right girl.'

'His mother was too possessive, that's his trouble. She dotes on him and one can see why. He has unusual charm. The

Marchesa kept him away from women; she didn't mind his boyfriends and he got into bad habits. One can't help feeling sorry for him — and for her. As a cavalry officer he was wildly extravagant. They are up to their eyes in debt.'

'How romantic! I don't believe any man is queer if he meets the right girl. Now I understand why I didn't take to the Marchesa.'

'She suffers acutely from his ostracism. With her delusions of grandeur she had pinned all her hopes to his worldly success — the last of the Buondelmonti! Now he can't even set foot in his club, the members cut him dead. The Marchesa puts a bold face on it though her former friends avoid her. It must be agony to go on pawning their precious heirlooms. Terence bought the tapestry with their coat of arms to pay one of her creditors.'

'She's more of a personality than I imagined. Now I'm almost tempted to accept her invitation to tea.'

'Obviously she hopes you'll make a convert of Aldo. I'd better chaperon you, dear. And Felix should be warned before you go.'

'Oh, Felix wouldn't mind in the least. He is too sure of himself to be jealous, and from what you tell me . . .'

'Come vuole cara, I disclaim responsibility. Aldo lives like a recluse on a lower floor of their palazzo. People say he has orgies there — I don't believe it. Terence and I have always stood by him. When he cut me in the street I scolded him: "You can't do that to me!" He smiled and kissed my hand. "I admire your pluck," he replied, and sent me some gorgeous lilies he couldn't afford. There's no doubt he has quality.'

The more Bella heard of Aldo, the more he titillated her imagination. Priscilla's Italian visitors were even more conventional than the old folks at home.

The few originals were English, German, Russian or French. The English were the most eccentric: they would take off their clothes and dance on the lawn if they felt inclined to do so. Florence affected them in unpredictable ways. The Russians behaved like characters in Dostoievsky. But Aldo was half a New Englander, which might account for his deviation from the average.

Priscilla escorted Bella to the sombre palace in a narrow street where the Marchesa had invited them to tea. The columned courtyard was worthy of Brunelleschi though its symmetry was marred by scattered mounds of wine casks exuding a musty odour. The Marchesa's apartment was equally musty: it had a moth-eaten air in the powdery twilight. The Marchesa herself was decidedly crepuscular as she drifted towards them like ectoplasm in a shawl. The lamps were too dim to illuminate more than a thigh or a shoulder of the bituminous canvases on the walls — 'the family Guercinos' she called them. Dimly they suggested martyrdoms.

'It was dear of you to visit a decrepit old creature like me,' she quavered. 'We were better off in Rome when my husband was chamberlain to His Majesty. Florence is rather a come-down after the Eternal City: no Quirinal, no Vatican! But the Buondelmonti belong to Florentine history. My son could tell you about them, a complicated saga. He has never been to the States; nor have I since I sailed from Salem at the age of six. But his English is as fluent as mine: we speak it together to keep in practice, for I'm apt to get rusty.'

Tea was a long time coming, and in the meantime the Marchesa asked if they would prefer *vin santo*, which stood in a dusty decanter beside her armchair.

She was pouring a potion for herself when a shrivelled crone staggered in with a tray too heavy for her. Priscilla went to her assistance while the Marchesa sipped her wine complacently. 'Where is Aldo?' she enquired.

'He promised to come but, as you know, he's shy. I'll send Fiammetta for him . . . Ah, there he is!'

Suddenly he stood at the door, tall, slender, broad-shouldered, with classical features except for his overripe lips. 'Antinous in person,' thought Bella, mesmerized by his appearance. She trembled all over when he kissed her hand. Aware that he had made a hit, his jet eyes sparkled.

'We were waiting for you, *birichino*. Where have you been?' his mother cooed.

'Riding in the Cascine as usual.'

'He's a regular daredevil on a horse. It makes me nervous.' Bella wondered how such a mother could have produced such a son. They had not one feature in common.

'Now you will be able to practise your English on pretty Mrs Overton. She's staying with Priscilla till she finds the ideal villa.'

'It's a pity we had to sell ours. We sold it to a Prato merchant who promptly pulled it down. It was rather decayed but the situation was spectacular. I'll show you an old print of it and I can show you the garden, what's left of it. The ilex grove and a few statues are still standing. With your husband's permission I could take you there in my pony cart.'

'No permission required. I follow my own sweet will.'

Bella was so fascinated by Aldo's face that she hardly listened to his words: his lips as he pronounced them were caressing. There was nothing effeminate about him — even Felix used eau-de-Cologne. She had always associated 'queers' with effeminacy — a la-di-da limpness and languor, flappings of the wrist and wrigglings of the little finger, as if waiting for a canary to perch on the tip of a manicured nail. Though his olive skin looked too smooth to need a razor and his raven hair had the sheen of lacquer his voice had a masculine resonance. His expression was wistful till he broke into a smile. He was flattered and amused by Bella's candour.

'You are really too handsome for a man,' she said. 'Why have we not met before?'

'Some day I'll tell you, when we get to know each other. No doubt you have heard from Priscilla: that I have been the victim of unkind gossip. I have lost many friends, but they were not real friends.'

'I hope we shall be real friends,' Bella gushed. He purred like a petted cat.

'I hope so too.'

75

Priscilla became embarrassed by Bella's concentration on Aldo: she paid no attention to the Marchesa or herself. The Marchesa watched them with an indulgent smile as they drew closer together. Her instinct had not failed her: the rendezvous was auspicious, Aldo's magnetism worked. She pressed Bella's hand with maternal warmth. 'I seldom leave my lair,' she said, 'but you must come back and visit us as often as you please. We Yankees should stick together.'

Bella reflected that in America the Marchesa would be a strange fish out of water. A lifetime in Italy had transformed her into a monstrous hybrid, whereas her son was Latin to the core.

Aldo escorted her down the smelly stairs and again her knees trembled when he bowed to kiss her hand. 'Promise me to return. You have done my poor mother so much good. She is very lonely, partly through my fault, and you have cheered her up immensely.'

'I'll return to see *you*,' said Bella, forbearing to add: 'your old mother be hanged!'

'What if the others prejudice you against me, or prejudice your husband?'

'My husband is immune to gossip. It was for my sake that he came to Florence instead of toiling in his father's office. Our marriage is based on mutual tolerance.'

'Thank you for this comforting assurance. I never needed it more. *A rivederla!*'

'How could anyone call him queer?' Bella remarked to Priscilla in the carriage. 'He seems to me perfectly normal.'

'Seems,' said Priscilla, 'but I'm afraid there's no smoke without fire. I don't want to get into your hubby's bad books.'

'It has been a refreshing surprise. One cannot help liking him but I can't say as much for his mamma. What is it about her that gives one goose-pimples?'

'I suspect it is due to the strain of making both ends meet. Aldo's incorrigibly extravagant. You should see the collection of silver trophies he won as a cavalry officer. His mother wanted to sell them, but they are the last thing he would agree to part with. She's always in and out of the pawnbroker's: it has given her a shifty expression. She had hoped for better days...'

Eventually Felix found a secluded villa on a hilltop above acres of vines and olives and, having bought it, he set to work remodelling it according to his standards of Tuscan proportion and American comfort. He discovered a hidden fresco here, a buried courtyard there, and looked forward to disinterring greater artefacts while shifting the main entrance and adding an extensive studio. Felix was to rebuild and Bella to furnish and decorate it. Internal walls were demolished to amplify space, for Bella visualized herself as queen of an autonomous region. She was too absorbed in the process of adaptation to devote much leisure to Aldo, though his image pursued her everywhere. There were times when she longed for a *tête-à-tête* with him, yet she was half afraid of seeing him alone. Their spontaneous communion of sympathy haunted her. She could hardly explain it to herself: nobody in Florence had appealed to her so vividly. While she had been captivated by his Renaissance physique, she fancied that his attraction was purely aesthetic, that of a living work of art. Often when she glanced at Felix it was Aldo's face that hovered before her eyes: his features were magically superimposed.

Gradually she got into the habit of stopping at his palace on the way home, under the pretext of showing him her latest 'find' and discussing it with him, or of consulting him about some detail of decoration. The fact that he was shunned by the *beau monde* added a piquancy to these impromptu visits. Cautiously he half-opened the door of his dingy apartment and, recognizing Bella, flung it wide open with a flashing smile of welcome.

Conversation flowed naturally between them, for Aldo's shyness was apocryphal. He interpreted Florence for her.

'When will you come up to our villa?' she asked.

'Whenever I am invited. Your husband might not welcome the intrusion of a social pariah.'

'Nonsense, my friends are his though we laugh at different jokes. He takes himself seriously as a down-to-earth American. What do you mean by "social pariah"? Are you quizzing?'

'Don't pretend you have not heard the ugly rumours. Priscilla must have told you.'

Bella flushed. 'I refused to listen.'

'Alas, they are true. I was kicked out of the army.'

'Don't tell me,' she breathed on a note of entreaty.

'Not tell you? If we are to be real friends — *Lei è tanto simpatica!* — I must put all my cards on the table at once. No cheating, no false pretences! I could not bear you to see me otherwise than I am.'

'Some things are better left unsaid. I'm afraid you will nip our friendship in the bud.'

All the same he had whetted her curiosity.

'I know you will understand,' he said after an electric pause. Bella leaned forward and laid her hand on his. First he told her about his giddy life as a cavalry officer.

'You must have been gorgeous in your uniform. Didn't lots of women fall in love with you?'

'One did, and that was what ruined me. Lady Gregson was already middle-aged with *des beaux restes* and plenty of money to preserve them. Her passion was insatiable and I could not respond. I was foolish ever to attempt it, but I had expensive tastes and she could be lavish. When she realized she was repulsive to me her caresses became vicious, obscene. She followed me and had me followed. It was the persecution of a frustrated fury. I suppose by way of reaction I fell into the arms of a young orderly, a Sicilian boy who had been initiated into the mysteries of pagan love by a German baron in Taormina. He offered himself to me and we had secret assignations. At first I struggled against temptation, but once I surrendered I could see no harm in it. After the suffocating embraces of that woman his clean contact was bracing. I had never experienced such rapture and it was not all on one side . . . Then Lady Gregson intercepted a letter which she stole from my coat pocket. It was

78

madly indiscreet, but then I was mad and took crazy risks on the Pincio and in the Colosseum . . .'

'Aldo, don't tell me more!'

'You must hear me to the end if you are not to condemn me. With the stolen letter Lady Gregson denounced me to my colonel and told all her friends and mine that I was a *finocchio*, a pervert. As the general in command was my godfather, he urged me to resign before I was court-martialled. I gave up my sword and parted from my favourite Arab mare which had won so many races. The disgrace prostrated my mother, but she is brave. As for me, I was near to suicide, but the young Sicilian made me want to live. You see I have opened my heart to you as to nobody else, not even to my mother. With her puritan background she would not understand: fortunately she was spared the details. Lady Gregson wrote to her: she tore up the letters as soon as she received them. Since then my old comrades reject me, even those who share my inclinations, perhaps because they do. Had I been caught in a brothel, it would have been marked to my credit. Well, I enjoyed my Roman Carnival while it lasted, the grand balls and suppers and hunts in the Campagna. Left to myself, I'm beginning to know myself.'

'Why do you tell me these things, Aldo? They must hurt.'

'Yes, there are times when I hate and despise myself. I am blinded with shame. Then I remember the great artists and poets who shared my failing, and that restores my self-respect.' His dark eyes lit up with a phosphorescent glow like those of a night bird. 'I tell you these things because you are the first person to offer me genuine sympathy. Having found a true friend, I wish to hide nothing from you.'

'They make no difference to my feeling for you, Aldo. Don't be afraid, I am not like Lady Gregson.'

Aldo laughed bitterly. 'You could not be. She was uniquely horrible.'

He entertained Bella with his fantastic anecdotes and witty mimicry; he saddened her with the pathos of his predicament.

He missed the camaraderie of his cavalry regiment.

Lady Gregson became a cathartic joke between them. 'As Lady Gregson used to say... When Lady Gregson followed me into the bathroom . . .' He was so funny about her that Bella sometimes suspected that she was a comic invention, as when she became coy over handling asparagus, or tried to seduce him with spinach between her front teeth, or offered to darn his socks to purloin them as souvenirs. And Bella would tease him about her: 'Perhaps she was really a lesbian?'

'She behaved like one in bed. Her loose mouth slobbered all over me, staining me with lipstick. I had to dry myself with an enormous towel, and even then something stuck like glue...'

But Bella never teased him about his private alcove, though the sight of a soldier loitering near the porter's lodge provoked an itch to do so. Of her husband she spoke as a nice but necessary nuisance. 'I guess we need each other in a practical way. Physically he leaves me cold. Perhaps it is my fault. I am happy enough just to sit and listen to you, dear Aldo.'

Indeed they were happy together, especially when they went out riding in the country. 'I forget my troubles on horseback. They return when I sit in a chair,' Aldo said. Felix was entirely occupied at the villa, so Bella was free to roam to her heart's content.

'Aren't you seeing too much of Aldo?' Priscilla inquired. 'After all, you are about the same age, a teeny bit older perhaps. Of course Felix has nothing to fear from a fairy but that won't stop tongues wagging. I implore you to be careful.'

'Live and let live is my motto. I look upon Aldo as my guardian angel.'

'I should say it's the other way round. He has everything to gain from your company. The Marchesa may hope it will whitewash him, but Florentines have long memories.'

'I don't care a fig for their malice. One of the reasons I came here was to escape from stifling convention.'

When the Villa Bella, as it was christened, became habitable she brought Aldo to see it. Felix was installed with his drawing board on the terrace. He was a sturdy fair-haired man of thirty-five, clean-shaven and reserved. He shook hands with Aldo in a brisk and casual manner, excusing himself from accompanying him indoors. He was planning to build a trap-door leading from his bedroom to Bella's below. Through this he could climb down a rope ladder for nocturnal visits. While he explained the convenience of this arrangement since he was addicted to snoring, Aldo could hardly repress a smile, but he complimented Felix on the amenity of the place. Its Tuscan restraint had been preserved, and a formal parterre was emerging above the *podere,* with a central fountain and zinnias between box hedges.

Bella was struck by the contrast between Aldo and her husband: Felix so square and practical in tweeds looked out of place, a crude interloper from the new world, whereas Aldo, with his lithe grace and aristocratic poise, appeared to belong to the villa as if he had been born there.

'How I wish we could live here together, what fun we might have!' Bella exclaimed.

'It would be idyllic, wouldn't it? We would ride and philosophize and comb the curio shops, and on winter evenings we would sit by the fire and dream . . .'

There was plenty of extra room, she reflected. If only Felix were different it might be arranged, with each in a separate compartment — a harmonious *ménage à trois.* Aldo would supply the poetry and Felix the solid prose. But without any comment she sensed that Felix was hostile. His New England features had hardened when she introduced him, and he had been barely civil. She sighed and clasped Aldo's hand. He returned her pressure and drew her fingers to his lips. *'Fata morgana,'* he murmured.

Often he called on her at teatime when Felix was out. His mere presence was a stimulant, even when he was in one of his despondent moods. He had bursts of gaiety but he was seldom cheerful: he depended on Bella to relieve his chronic melancholy. Once when his silence was more persistent than usual as he sat gazing gloomily into the fireplace, she noticed a look she had not seen on his face, though its classical outline had become so familiar. It was like the moral equivalent of physical fatigue. She asked him what was the matter.

'Oh, nothing in particular,' he faltered.

'But I can see that something is worrying you, Aldo. Your depression is infectious. I am here to help you. What is the use of a friend you can't confide in?'

His lips quivered in hesitation. 'I should not have come here today,' he broke out. 'Why should I inflict my petty troubles on you? I only want you to see me when I'm carefree.'

'Nonsense, don't you trust my discretion? Out with it, let me hear the worst! Together we may solve your problems.'

'It's all so sordid. Mamma is overdrawn again and we haven't a penny to pay up with. She has tried to sell our Guercinos but nobody wants them. She has already sold the Duccio for a fraction of its value.'

He twisted his long fine fingers in distress. 'It is so deeply humiliating. The last of the Buondelmonti!'

Bella was in a quandary. It would be simple to offer him a cheque but Felix was certain to find out since it would be drawn on their common account, which would be difficult to explain. Moreover, Terence was their banker, and he would tell Priscilla . . .

'My pearl necklace,' she remembered in a rush of inspiration. Felix would never notice: she wore it so seldom. She preferred her amber beads. 'Wait a moment,' she said, and ran to fetch the necklace her grandfather had given her as a débutante. She placed it in a gold filigree box she had bought on the Ponte Vecchio.

Aldo was still staring vacantly into the fire when she tiptoed beside him, palpitating to relieve his anxiety.

'Here are some pearls, Aldo mio. Take them and sell them, dear. They ought to help.'

'Oh Bella, carissima, you shouldn't!' he protested. 'You are too good to me, too generous. What have I done to deserve them?' His cheeks were flushed, his eyes glittered with tears, and while protesting he snatched the box with a tremulous hand.

'Won't you take a peep at them? Suppose I am pulling your leg?'

In dismay he drew out the symmetrically matched pearls and held them up to the lamplight.

'Exquisite! They are so much yours, carissima, that I haven't the heart to accept them. No, really, you will regret your sacrifice, and then . . . I may lose your friendship.'

Fearing that Felix might butt in at any moment, Bella grew impatient. 'Stop fussing and take them,' she insisted.

With a rueful smile of apology he slipped her gift into his pocket. Even through his glow of gratitude Bella was alarmed by the hint of a sneer almost evil as he clasped her hand and covered it with kisses. Bella withdrew it with a faint shiver.

She had glimpsed another Aldo, whose grimace she would not easily forget. Far from repelling her, however, it gave a new depth to his elusive character. It was a depth she longed to probe, an atavistic inheritance.

'Tell me about your ancestors, Aldo. I've been wanting to ask since your mother mentioned your knowledge of their history.'

'They go very far back — to the time when they were feudal barons. Dante blamed the Buondelmonti for the Florentine factions in the thirteenth century. He wished they had been drowned in the Ema before coming to Florence, and others have wished it since then. The Florentines destroyed their castle of Montebuono and compelled them to move into the city. One Buondelmont produced the first map of the Aegean and its islands, but my favourite ancestor was murdered after his wedding on Easter day in 1216.'

'And we're so proud of our Pilgrim fathers and Mayflower descendants! Why was the murdered Buondelmonte your favourite?'

'His fate was so tragic. To appease the rival factions a priest induced him to get engaged to a daughter of the Amidei, but he never kept the appointment with her relatives to sign the contract. They swore to avenge the insult. In the meantime he had fallen in love with Fina dei Donati and signed another contract with her mother. After the wedding the young couple rode across the river to the bride's new house on Piazza Santa Trinita, Buondelmonte in a silver embroidered jerkin, Fina in bridal white crowned with a wreath of roses. Their mothers followed in litters with a retinue of knights. On Via Por Santa Maria a gang rushed out of the Amidei palace and Buondelmonte was attacked with a mace and stabbed to death. The shrieks of the bride were echoed by those of the jilted girl peering down from the tower of the Lambertesca palace. By evening the whole city was in an uproar. The corpse was laid on an open bier, the head resting on the lap of his bride. Thus the living and the dead were carried through the streets with the cry: "A Buondelmonte! To the rescue!" In those times we were always in the thick of the fray. Though nobles we were Guelphs and fought the Ghibellines. Our name was a battle-cry!'

'You ought to write this down for posterity. Nobody could do it better. You make one actually see what you describe.'

'You flatter me, Bella, but I have no literary skill. I can only remember our domestic tragedies. The rest is rather drab. We have become like the *poveri vergognosi* of Venice.'

Bella thought Felix might be interested in the history of Aldo's family. 'It is full of melodrama,' she remarked.

'Too full, I guess,' he retorted. 'I wish you saw less of that guy: he gives me the willies. I tried to be civil for your sake but honestly I don't like him. And people are talking.'

'How do you know?'

'I do know, that's the point. I object to being made a fool of.'

'Why should I drop a good friend for a bunch of backbiting tabbies? Nobody could accuse Aldo of compromising me.'

'I'm not so sure of that.'

Had Priscilla been repeating malicious gossip? In a fit of

perversity Bella invited Aldo and his mother to dinner the next evening. 'An intimate family party, just the four of us. How nice!' the Marchesa exclaimed.

The dinner was not a success. Felix, never garrulous, left the Marchesa to keep the ball rolling during the meal, which she did with the bravado of an old war-horse. Aldo was subdued; Bella tense under a mask of nonchalance. She had much to say, but she could not say it while her husband glowered across the table. The Marchesa's affability was wasted on him. The flickering candles seemed to mock his malaise; the wine failed to mellow his temper.

After coffee was served Bella led Aldo to the piano in the adjoining studio. They practised a new song as they had often done before, and while he hummed the tune to her accompaniment she whispered that Felix was upset about their intimacy.

'He looked angry, but how can we appease him?'

'Why not take him aside for a heart to heart talk? It isn't as if we were having an affair.'

'I'm afraid he is on the side of the enemy. He has never approved of our friendship and now he is jealous.'

'What's the name of that song?' the Marchesa called from the drawing-room.

'*En bateau*, Mamma.'

'A boat, that's just what I'm thinking of,' Felix muttered.

'It's simply sweet. Do give us an encore.' Aldo lowered his voice while she repeated the opening chords: 'If they part us now, they might as well kill me.'

His expression was so miserable that Bella caught both his hands. 'I will never let that happen.' She had stopped playing and she spoke loud enough to be overheard: 'I'll always be your friend.'

Felix stalked in to see Aldo drop her hands like hot pokers. He was white with rage. The party ended in monosyllables between prickly silences.

'Thanks for the cosy evening,' gushed the Marchesa. 'The

85

soufflé was delicious. I can only offer you a *casalinga* meal, but we must repeat this happy occasion. Just the four of us *chez moi.*'

They parted frigidly. Felix said nothing: he would not shake hands with Aldo, or kiss Bella goodnight.

After midnight Bella was wakened by the arrival of Felix beside her bed with a lighted candle. He told her gruffly that he was going back to America. She could accompany him if she liked: if not, she would never see him again.

'You have the rest of the night to think it over,' he said.

It was impossible to make him understand a platonic attachment between a man and a woman. In spite of Aldo's reputation appearances were against her since that incident at the piano. The mere suspicion of a flirtation with a fairy, however false, was an outrage to his masculine pride.

Bella had a sharp struggle to weigh her passionate sympathy for Aldo against the loss of a dependable husband, the pros of romance and the cons of matrimony. As the day dawned she decided reluctantly to sacrifice Aldo to Felix. She would telephone him in the morning, begging him to trust her, promising to return as soon as possible. Surely he would understand that divorce was out of the question. After a reasonable interval Felix was bound to cool off.

Felix's jaw was stubbornly set when she announced her painful decision: he forbade her to telephone Aldo and the letter she sent him by hand was never delivered.

Priscilla popped round in the role of Job's comforter. An elopement with Aldo, as the gossips prophesied, would be a disaster for all concerned, she said. Bella had so many sound reasons for staying with Felix, whereas Aldo could never be satisfactory to live with: he was notoriously too far gone in another direction. And from what she knew of Bella, who was ultra-normal, his friendship would never be a substitute for the real thing. Far better to let the rumours die down.

Bella protested that the beauty of her relation with Aldo was that it went deeper and wider than the sexual thing, but nobody could fathom such a spiritual affinity, least of all Felix. She burst into tears.

86

Even Priscilla believed, like Felix, that the Marchesa and Aldo were scheming to retrieve his social position at Bella's expense. The Marchesa talked as if she had found a goldmine. Everybody had heard of the pearl necklace Bella had given him . . .

Bella's conscience smote her all the way across the Atlantic. It preyed on her mind that Aldo, who had filled her life with sunshine, should waste his life in the solitude of his dingy apartment, brooding on her desertion. She moped in her state cabin while Felix played games with the fellow passengers she shunned as trivial vulgarians. Why had she been such a cowardly slave to convention? How Aldo must despise her!

Back in Boston Bella was fêted like a returning prodigal. She enjoyed herself so much that the image of distant Aldo began to fade. She had always lived in and for the present moment; it was her outstanding American trait. Occasionally she sent Aldo a tender note with a little present, some novelty that might appeal to his sense of humour.

After several months Felix was convinced that she had outgrown her embarrassing infatuation. Aldo's name was never mentioned between them. Towards summer both were eager to put the finishing touches to the Villa Bella, whose Cinquecento foundations had been impeccably restored. Felix had removed later obstructions from the original *cortile* and the spacious vaulted rooms. It was already a 'show place' much grander than the Villa Sperry.

But the very air of Florence revived memories of Aldo, of their country rides and intimate discussions by the fireside. Bella's craving for him was dumb, but Felix must have had an intuition of it for he warned her to avoid any contact with the Buondelmonti. If she encountered the Marchesa or her son she was not to recognize them.

Aldo had been so poignant an element of Bella's Florence and its local colour that she missed him wherever she went. The villa seemed forlorn without his visits, the piano where he had sung so often beside her was a standing reproach. She never practised nowadays.

Longing yet dreading to see him, she drove daily into the town, yet she never happened to meet him. Then, after a fortnight, his slim grey figure advanced towards her in the Via Tornabuoni as she was about to enter her carriage. He slackened his pace and stopped, and his lustrous eyes gazed into hers mournfully, hypnotically. Bella felt suddenly frozen. She looked through him without a sign of recognition, and he stood gazing towards her with tears in his eyes till she drove away.

Next morning Felix came whistling into her bedroom while she sat sipping her *café au lait* among her pink pillows. He paused at the open window and examined the view with an air of curious elation. 'I have just received a telephone message,' he said curtly. 'The Marchese Aldo shot and killed himself last night. And a good thing too.'

'It was I who killed him,' she mused with a pang of luxurious guilt. He must have loved her more deeply than she realized. She might have saved him with a touch, a regretful smile. Eventually she came to regard his suicide as a supreme compliment, and when she was stared at as a *femme fatale* on the Via Tornabuoni she held her head high. But she never knew that his Sicilian Ganymede had left him for a Swiss manufacturer of watches.

Flora's Lame Duck

Nobody knew where he had sprung from, and indeed there was something spectral about his limping after Flora in the back streets of San Frediano, for he seldom appeared with her in the Via Tornabuoni where he would have been conspicuous. Alabaster-pale with piercing jet eyes and a mop of raven hair, he might have been Flora's son by a Latin lover.

It was rumoured that Flora had rescued him from a concentration camp when she was working for the Red Cross at the end of the last war, that he had been left an orphan stricken with polio. But he was too self-effacing to kindle much curiosity among Flora's frivolous acquaintances. At her cocktail parties he kept aloof from the crowd, impassive and immobile, if he happened to be in the room.

'Ugo is very shy,' she explained. 'Though not socially inclined he needs to be near me.'

His mournful eyes followed Flora as she poured out drinks for her guests. Now and then he would limp towards her and whisper something in her ear. She smiled at him with gracious condescension. Flora had always been gregarious: at certain hours she liked to be surrounded by laughing chattering people. Which made it all the stranger that she should have taken so taciturn a protégé to live with her. One could hardly imagine that they had much in common. A maternal sympathy, perhaps, for at nineteen Ugo still seemed adolescent.

'Like something the cat has brought in,' remarked her old crony Ronald Lipson with his vintage malice. 'Makes me shudder. But one must put up with Flora's charities.'

Feeling sorry for that fish out of water, I joined him in his corner by the Japanese screen, but he was difficult to engage in conversation. When I introduced myself as a school friend of Flora's all he could say in Italian was: 'Isn't she beautiful? The Lord has been merciful to me. She is my guardian angel.'

In her early forties Flora was still slender and girlish in her movements, simply yet stylishly clad without ornaments. Her carefully made-up face produced an impression of modern sophistication (Paris, London, New York) rather than of beauty. Having divorced a rich alcoholic husband she took up various charitable works to assert her individuality. It was assumed that Ugo belonged to that category. Flora's charities were personal yet selfless: she went out of her way to find congenial occupations for the disabled and under-privileged despite a distaste for physical contact with them. It was not easy to conceal her horror of the deformed. Elmer Stoddard, the one man she deeply loved, was married in New York, but his wife was suffering from an incurable disease and he had not the heart to abandon her. The specialists predicted that she could not last much longer. She was kept alive on sedatives.

Elmer implored Flora to be patient. 'We shall soon make up for lost time,' he assured her. All the time they were separated was lost for Flora: only her charities helped her to fill the great gap. It seemed cruel to hope for his wife to die, but in her predicament euthanasia would be a blessing.

Flora had been tempted to linger in New York for Elmer's sake until her frustration became intolerable. There was but little consolation in casual assignations, for Elmer, being full-blooded, endeavoured to make love to her whenever they met. The image of his bedridden wife hovered malignantly between them and Flora suspected that she had the clairvoyance of the dying. A conventional believer in matrimony, she would not yield to Elmer's entreaties for a premature consummation. So she reconciled herself to more anxious waiting. Meanwhile she decided to return to Florence where she had struck roots with her former husband before the war.

Her Florentine friends clasped her to their bosoms and those among them who had been ardent Fascists welcomed her oblivious of bygone differences. The most ardent had been Anglo-American countesses who had deified the *Duce* as a symbol of heroic virility: some of them still cherished his photograph in secret. Several had been impoverished by the war, and these were the most eager to entertain her at their country estates which, after an esurient fortnight in England, seemed to be flowing with milk and honey.

Flora threw open her elegant apartment above the Arno to her polyglot côterie with the profuse hospitality of her pre-war period. None could forget those parties where so many marriages had been arranged, and again Flora revelled in the role of matchmaker. She had found husbands for spinsters and wives for bachelors — another reason for her warm reception by couples to whose infants she had been a fairy godmother. Seeing her again immaculate and unchanged, they hoped she would persevere on behalf of their offspring. The younger generation looked towards America as the goal of their ambitions. They had long been deprived of Jazz, and the records Flora had brought from Manhattan excited their naïve enthusiasm. But the nostalgic tunes of the thirties were still the favourites with Flora's generation. Again, as before the war, an undulating group besieged the piano where Ronald Lipson regaled them with the lyrics of Cole Porter and Noël Coward. Ronnie knew most of them by heart and he sang them with the right intonations while others joined the chorus. Flora was reminded poignantly of Elmer when he crooned 'Some day he'll come along, the man I love, And he'll be big and strong, the man I love . . .'

It was the return of a Lady Bountiful who could solve everybody's problems except her own — her engagement to a man still tethered to a dying wife, and her subsequent responsibility for a limping waif.

Though he had been cured of polio Ugo was morbidly conscious of his deformity. He feared that Flora was ashamed of being seen with him. 'I feel I'm a terrible encumbrance,' he told her.

'Nonsense, you should be thinking of a career. At your age there are so many to choose from. When you have chosen you may count on my assistance.'

In feeding and clothing and sending him to study English at the British Institute she hoped he would discover a congenial profession. He had a talent for drawing which she encouraged by introducing him to a couple of artists who invited him to their studio and allowed him to draw from their models. Flora supplied him with abundant painting materials, delighted that he had found an innocuous hobby. Tactfully she respected his unwillingness to display his first efforts. 'You may show them to me when you feel you have something to be proud of,' she said.

'I should like to paint your portrait,' he replied. 'but I'm not good enough yet. I want to pour my love into the picture like the Mediterranean flowing into the Atlantic.'

Flora smiled as he prattled on with glittering eyes. He made sketches of her while she sat over her embroidery, and she would have been astonished at the result, for to her head and shoulders he added a naked figure with pear-shaped breasts and a forest of pubic hair intertwined with tendrils of ivy and bulbous lilies.

Considering her affection for Florence, Flora was strangely indifferent to the visual arts though she had a vague penchant for artists in general. Ugo hummed happily over his sketchbook. Ever and anon he moistened his large lips with a pointed tongue and his black eyes scrutinized her so intensely that Flora was disconcerted. It had not crossed her mind that he might fall in love with her but gradually she was forced to realize that this was happening. Never having experienced intimacy with a woman he was peculiarly susceptible to Flora's attractions. 'You are so beautiful,' he sighed, 'it makes me despair. I feel like a worm beside you.'

'Don't be silly,' she replied. 'You're simply sweet but you are a baby compared to me. And I have no pretence to beauty.'

'You have been so kind to me, too kind. You have shown me

a new world. How can I express my gratitude? Have you guessed how deeply I love you?'

'Be sensible, Ugo. Remember your age and mine, think of the difference.'

Ugo's eyes filled with tears. 'I cannot feel the difference, except that I'm a cripple.'

'You should regard your lameness as a distinction. Many famous people have been lame. Lord Byron for instance.'

As he had never heard of Byron Flora gave him a volume of his poems. No social introduction could have been as effective. He pored over the poems with rapture and Byron became a cult. Now he wore an open shirt with his velveteen jacket and attempted to emulate his hero by learning to swim in the Arno. He developed his breast strokes rapidly and while swimming forgot his deformity. Though his black eyebrows were gathered together above his nose he fancied that his features resembled those of the poet.

Flora's friends noticed a marked improvement in Ugo's physique when she took him to Forte dei Marmi for the summer. She had rented a small villa with a garden near the sea where she could indulge in the same social round as in the city within easy reach of canasta-playing neighbours. Ugo clung to her in private but in public he remained equally remote with his Byronic pose of vague mystery and disdain. People might think what they pleased but nothing Ugo said could compromise their relationship. He stood discreetly in the background, *a cavalier servente* at Flora's beck and call.

'After the hell she went through with her husband it's nice for Flora to have a young creature in attendance.'

'But what a creature! I wouldn't trust him round the corner. Half-boy, half-man, and not enough of either. He's getting a bit above himself. Flora gives him too much rope.'

His presence, even in the background, irritated the men who wanted to flirt with her. Which suited Flora, determined to be faithful to Elmer in thought, word and deed. Apart from assurances that he was alive and well, Elmer's letters brought little solace while his wife was kept barely alive by the miracles of modern medicine. In spite of her sociable routine at Forte Flora found it increasingly difficult to be patient. Elmer embodied her ideal of a staunch compatriot whose supreme sanity she could always bank on. His utter wholesomeness was perhaps his principal charm: his very sweat was perfume to her nostrils. In his last letter he had quoted Walt Whitman: 'I am to think of you when I sit at night alone, I am to wait, I do not doubt I am to meet you again, I am to see to it that I do not lose you.' Elmer's was the 'robust American love' celebrated by Whitman. Flora would fly back to New York as soon as he summoned her after the funeral. Both she and Elmer would be rejuvenated by a peripatetic honeymoon. Elmer had never been to Italy and Flora looked forward to acting as his guide and mentor.

Ugo was never mentioned in her letters though he monopolized more of her attention than she cared to admit even to herself. During the summer at Forte they swam together all morning and lay on a strip of sand with towels and rugs, novels and magazines and a picnic basket. Flora read in English to Ugo and he read in Italian to her with playful interruptions and dissertations. In the afternoon Flora relaxed for a siesta under a mosquito net in her cool shuttered bedroom while Ugo sat outside on the terrace under a canvas awning... Now and then he crept indoors to peep at her. He was restless and the sight of her made him more so. As he was barefooted Flora could not hear him while he stood gazing at her with bated breath. Her eyes were blindfold while his gloated on the curves of her naked body. He longed to leap under the net and snuggle in beside her, but he crept stealthily out of the room with all his senses on fire. To melt into that sumptuous flesh had now become his obsession. He staggered back to the beach to cool himself in the sea, but the salt water failed to calm his raging fever. He resolved to keep away from Flora at siesta-time lest he could not resist the impulse to ravish her. It was difficult enough to control his emotion when she sat beside him.

94

'What's the matter, dear?' she asked with tender concern.

'I'm afraid you would not understand.'

'Aren't you happy here? Tell me what is upsetting you.'

'I'm only too happy to be with you, I can't express it. But I want more love than you could give a wretch like me. I'm afraid I'm repulsive to you.'

'You are mistaken, Ugo. Just look at yourself in the mirror.'

'I can only look at you, Madonna Flora. Every day you become more beautiful. And you are all I have in the world.'

'Nonsense, dear. At your age the world is your oyster.' She patted his cheek maternally.

He siezed her hands and kissed them, and she could not help noticing the bulge below his belt. The sudden realization that his senses were inflamed embarrassed and alarmed her. She had been serenely unconscious of his masculinity and now he forced it upon her notice. His hands were in his trouser pockets when he spoke to her, his eyes narrowing and then widening as if to hypnotize her. And against her will she was slowly hypnotized.

When the long hot day was over and they sat on the terrace in deck-chairs Ugo's face seemed all aglow towards her, pale under the sunburnt cheeks, his whole body trembling. 'Please do not let me spend another night alone,' he implored her. Staggering forward from the shadows, he leaned over her with ravenous lips. Spontaneously her bare arms drew his face down to hers and it was a repetition of the old, old story. The pressure of Ugo's lips opened a hidden crater of bubbling lava. Ugo took advantage of the eruption to undress Flora with frantic fingers and Flora, half-swooning, submitted to his volcanic embraces. He transmitted his juvenile ardour to her languid limbs, and the flow of his pent-up emotion was like the moon that turns the tides. Proud of shattering her prudent reserve, Ugo became exuberantly cheerful. He laughed and sang and recovered his hearty appetite. *'Parlami d'amore, Mariù,'* he sang operatically.

Flora had felt she was humouring a sick child but she could

not deny that the experience had been pleasurable. It was an age since her senses had been so voluptuously stirred but it was a matter of the senses merely, her mind scarcely entered into it. This was so distinct from her desire for Elmer that her conscience was clear. She could see no harm in her response to the poor boy's craving — on the contrary. Something of the kind was bound to happen sooner or later, she reflected, and it might have happened sooner considering the unsuspected flame of Ugo's temperament. It was flattering to be adored by a creature so much younger but she did not intend to let him renew the bombardment.

She had not reckoned with his stubborn will. Having tasted honey he was gluttonous for more. Flora made excuses, feigned indisposition. 'Be a good boy. There is a season for everything. Run away and leave me alone!'

But he slipped off his clothes and paid no attention to her feeble protests. Gripping and enfolding her in his brawny arms, he hugged her to his hairy chest until, panting and gasping, she gave up the unequal struggle. He sucked her nipples and nibbled her armpits. 'Stop it, you little tiger!' she cried. But he only stopped her mouth with his own while massaging her mound of Venus. 'You are all mine!' he whispered triumphantly.

'Gently, gently, you hurt!'

'I want to wound you with love.' He who had seemed so wan and listless was insatiable. 'Love me with your lips, your tongue, your teeth,' he pleaded.

'Enough is enough: let me sleep!' she replied wearily, pushing him off the pillow. He soon dozed off after his strenuous exertions, to renew them after dawn.

How absurd it was really, she mused, and how undignified. Flora was annoyed with herself for letting compassion get the better of her. She must be more severe with Ugo in future. That the young were seduced by their elders struck her as a popular fallacy, for she had had no intention of being seduced by this boy. But he was indomitably persistent. If she complained of a headache he said, 'Let me kiss it away!' And his kisses were invariably a prelude to more substantial endearments.

She persuaded Ersilia, her maid, to move into the next bedroom as a chaperon. Ersilia resented Ugo's appropriation of her *Signora*. She called him *lo zoppo* and repeated the proverb *'chi va con lo zoppo impara a zoppicare'*, which could be paraphrased as 'bad company contaminates the good.' However, as she slept like a log she never heard Ugo's nocturnal forays into the *Signora's* bed or the crescendo of vibrations that ensued. She pretended not to know how far he had gone with her.

He could hardly have gone much further. Despite her resolutions Flora frequently succumbed to his blandishments. She saw him as the incarnation of a pagan satyr, and he made her feel pagan too, with his musky smell and his primitive cries of ecstasy, at first sipping, then gulping her like a beaker of heady wine, pouring his wild essence through her veins until she sank back with the moan of a ravished nymph. A dreamless sleep followed with Ugo's tousled head on her bosom. He was still there when Ersilia came with coffee in the morning. Ersilia was startled. 'For shame!' she shouted. 'Cover yourself decently and go back to your own room.'

'I'm quite comfortable here, thank you. And why should I cover the best part of me? At least it does not limp. Now bring me an extra cup and a plate of peaches.'

'I only accept commands from the *Signora*.'

Flora quietly ordered another cup for Ugo as if it were nothing out of the ordinary.

'He will have to fetch it himself. This is scandalous. I'm leaving. I have my reputation to consider. The neighbours will gossip.'

'Let everybody mind his own business. Why shouldn't Ugo share my bed? Stop fussing.'

Ersilia was so fond of the *Signora* that after perfunctory grumbling she changed her mind when Flora raised her wages. After all the *Signora* was a foreigner with an exotic outlook.

Though she never went to Mass she was generous to the poor. Nobody ever appealed to her in vain. She had helped Ersilia's family and paid for her old mother's kidney operation. So she stayed on, smothering her indignation with the lame interloper.

The scene with Ersilia cleared the air between them. Flora appeared less often with Ugo in public, on the beach or at cocktail parties. By day he was studious and retiring, but by night he was the same predatory lover.

'Where's Ugo?' a neighbour might ask out of casual curiosity.

'How should I know? Busy working, I expect. I seldom see him nowadays . . .'

'What sort of work?'

'He paints and writes poetry.'

The subject was dropped since her neighbours were interested in neither. 'Flora has always specialized in lame ducks,' as Ronald Lipson remarked.

Even in bed with Ugo it never crossed Flora's mind that she was being unfaithful to Elmer. Elmer was on a higher plane more spiritual than physical, and on this lofty summit she was faithful to him in thought, if not in deed. At the back of her mind she was always conscious of this special affinity. Though they had never lived together she knew him through and through: he was a rock of friendship as well as an ideal mate.

In spite of her association with Ugo she could not take him seriously as a male. With his sobs and sighs and gushes of emotion he was subconsciously feminine: his masculinity was superficial, it could not penetrate her deepest core. She had never spoken to him about Elmer.

While dreaming Ugo had called her 'Mamma', which revealed that he regarded her as a mother as well as a mistress, and she felt a mother's responsibility towards him. Now he wanted her in the daytime as well as at night, and he wept when she refused, however kindly. His demands had become oppressive, a sort of moral blackmail. There was something diseased about his turbulent lust: he was becoming vicious. Instead of soothing her senses he exasperated them, reminding her ironically of those sex machines on sale in Scandinavia, reducing her to an object of evacuation. She felt numb when she was not hostile, and as indifferent to his embraces as to those of the divorced husband who had only made love to her when he was drunk.

Mortified by her apathy, Ugo persevered in futile efforts to stimulate her till Flora burst out laughing.

Swiftly he drew away from her, offended and bewildered. 'Why do you laugh?' he asked her.

'If you could see yourself you would laugh too. You are such an acrobat. Isn't it rather tiring? Wouldn't it be better to go swimming in the sea?'

Ugo fell silent. He watched her in dismay, for he had little sense of humour where sex was concerned. He had been intensely serious, and proud of his conquest. 'So you do not love me!' he gasped.

'Did I ever say that I loved you? I feel affection for you but that is different. I could not bear to see you unhappy, and you looked so miserable.'

'I am much more miserable now.'

It was blackmail, sheer blackmail. He threatened suicide and cut his wrists to prove that he was in earnest. Again Flora had to play the role of comforter, and he would not be comforted without her physical surrender. He loosened his bandages and bled copiously over her blouse. Ersilia screamed at the sight of it and wanted to call a doctor. *'Questo zoppo ci porta la iella,'* she exlaimed — 'this lame one brings us bad luck.' But the cuts were not deep and Flora bandaged them while Ersilia praised her pluck. Shaking a finger at Ugo she shrilled: 'Stop frightening us. This is no way for a guest to behave. And the poor *Signora* has treated you with such kindness. Try to be more considerate in future.'

Ugo calmed down when they returned to the apartment in Florence. He took up his painting again and Flora posed for him, but not as he wished in the nude. The result was admired by her friends. Undoubtedly he showed promise, they agreed, he could catch a certain likeness. Flora persuaded others to pose for him with the prospect of holding an exhibition.

At last the longed-for telegram arrived. Elmer asked Flora to join him in New York. His wife having 'passed away' he was free to remarry. Flora rushed out to buy her ticket and started packing. Ugo was banished from her mind: of course she would provide for him and he could stay on in the apartment for the time being, Ersilia would remain in charge. Flora's friends were invited to an impromptu farewell party.

When Ugo returned from the studio Ronald was playing 'The man I love' on the drawing-room piano and the canasta-players were toasting Flora and wishing her a happy voyage. Everybody was kissing her and cracking jokes about wedding bells. Flora stood flushed and radiant in their midst. Ugo peered at the festive gathering with haggard eyes, invisible to the crowd of merrymakers. He had been surprised to notice a couple of suitcases beside the front entrance. 'What does it mean?' he asked Ersilia.

'Haven't you heard?' she replied with a sly grin. 'The *Signora* is going home to be married.'

'Impossible!' he cried, 'this cannot be true. She has told me nothing about it.'

'Her friends in the drawing-room are celebrating the glad news. Her essential bags are packed; she leaves tomorrow by the night train to Paris.'

Reeling under the shock, Ugo had an impulse to shout: 'She's my woman. She belongs to me!' But he spun round and fled, his brain in a chaotic whirl. His whole horizon had collapsed as in an earthquake. 'She's going and soon she will be gone,' he muttered, 'and what will become of me now?'

He was appalled by Flora's deception: everything he had thought safe in the world came crashing down. He had no other friend in the world, nor any next of kin. She had picked him up and dropped him like a soiled handkerchief. The woman was heartless, but he would not allow her to desert him so easily. He wandered through the streets in a trance of despair: how could he stop her? It occurred to him that perhaps Ersilia had invented the whole thing just to spite him, yes, that was plausible since she had always hated him.

Half gliding, half hopping with nervous apprehension, he made his way back to the apartment for an explanation. Ersilia need not announce him for he had the keys. He found Flora resting in her bedroom after the party, her eyes blindfolded as usual against the light. Ugo was dazed by the beautiful curves of her body as if he had never seen it before. He knelt beside her and deliriously kissed her hands.

'So you have come,' she said. 'I was wondering where you had gone. We missed you at my farewell party.'

'Farewell for whom?'

'I have been recalled to New York by my fiancé. At last we are free to marry.'

So it was true. All that Ugo had been prepared to say stuck in his throat. He gazed at her piteously like a beaten dog, his pallor alarmingly bloodless. 'Why did you not warn me?' he wailed. 'Have I proved unworthy of your confidence?'

'I did not want to hurt your feelings. You are so terribly sensitive. The fact is I was engaged even before we met, but my fiancé was tied to another woman. It was an impossible situation and I had no desire to discuss it with you or with anyone else. What did you ever know about my real self?'

'I knew you as a woman. You made a man of me. Does that mean nothing to you, nothing at all?'

'It is nothing beside my engagement to a man of my own age and nationality.'

'You have played with me like a puppet; and now what am I to do? You have been everything to me. How can I exist without you?'

'Don't be melodramatic. I shan't be gone indefinitely — and of course we'll keep in touch. You might even come to America, but it is too early to decide. Ersilia can look after you

101

in the meantime, and I'll give you the money for living expenses if that's what is worrying you. We must be practical and realistic, *non è vero?*'

'So you only gave yourself to me out of pity. Have you told your fiancé about that or would you prefer me to tell him? It would make a pretty story: The American beauty and the crippled pauper, to read on your honeymoon.'

'Yes, Ugo, I pitied you sincerely with all my heart. But you pitied yourself much more. I had hoped to cure you of it as you were cured of polio, but I see that I have failed. Your self-pity is self-destructive, your lameness has gone to your head. You insisted on being loved when you only loved yourself. You needed someone to whom you could hitch your ego and I was that unlucky person. You repay me with bitter insolence. I can leave you without regret.'

'You cannot deny that you enjoyed our nights together. Your American fiancé will make you miss them.'

She gave him a resounding slap. 'Get out of my sight. *Fuori!*'

He spat at her: *'Sporca puttana!'*

He tried to climb on top of her and there was a furious struggle. Flora rang for Ersilia but there was no answer for she had sent her on some final errands. *'Puttana, puttana!'* he hissed. But Flora was the stronger and she sent him flying. *'Storpio maligno! Via!'*

Cursing her, he tottered out of the bedroom where he had made love to her so often. If only he had a revolver! He must make do with a substitute. In the kitchen he chose the sharpest knife he could find and hid it under his jacket.

'Back again! This is insufferable. Once and for all go away, or I'll call the carabinieri!'

'Addio!' he muttered, and plunged the knife between her breasts. To make doubly certain he withdrew it and thrust it violently into her belly and thighs, drenching the sheets in blood, then wiping the blade on her hair. He had intended to cut his throat but it seemed too messy, so he replaced the knife in the kitchen and threw himself out of the window.

It looked as if all the lilies of Florence, male, female and strictly botanical, had assembled for Flora's funeral in the Episcopalian church. The massed tuberoses round the coffin were more overpowering than fumes of incense. All Flora's friends and many who had scarcely known her filled the pews with streaming eyes and drawn expressions. Their sobs and sniffles were muted by the organ where Ronald Lipson, who had fortified himself with gin, played 'I'll see you again' as a voluntary while the congregation waited for the coffin to be carried up the aisle. The coffin was surprisingly small, as if Flora had shrunk from loss of blood. Ersilia wept hysterically and had to be supported when, swaying to her knees, she placed a bouquet of immortelles on the shiny lid of the coffin. Having taken an extra swig of gin from his hip-flask, a relic of Prohibition days, Ronnie played 'The man I love' pianissimo, in lieu of a hymn. Nobody thought of poor Elmer, who was expecting Flora in New York. In any case, he would have been an outsider.

The officiating clergyman paid eloquent tribute to Flora's philanthropic heart and democratic spirit. She had done her utmost to comfort and alleviate the distressed. It was no exaggeration to assert that she had fallen a victim to her boundless charity. An angel on earth, she had joined the angels in Heaven, a shining example to all of us. Though her charity began at home she never let it stay there. When her care for the handicapped was mentioned some were reminded of Ugo, her last lame duck.

'I always mistrusted him,' said Ronnie. 'To my mind he was a warning against indiscriminate charity, whatever the parson may say.'

The owner of Flora's apartment on the Arno was afraid that nobody would want to rent it since the sensational murder, but he was mistaken. He was flooded with requests to visit it, and Flora's bedroom in particular. He told me that he had been offered considerable sums by fetishists for the bloodstained sheets. Unfortunately the sheets had gone to the laundry, but Ersilia sold the kitchen knife for the price of a brand-new radio.

The Soul's Gymnasium

'If you are so keen on Italian gardens, the Hercules villa at Bellosguardo is an absolute must.'

'Is it open to the public?'

'Once or twice a week. The tourist agency will tell you, or your hotel porter. There are guided tours of the best gardens around Florence.'

'But I want enough leisure to browse and take photographs. On a guided tour I'd feel frustrated. The blue-haired matrons and blue-jeaned girls would spoil the atmosphere.'

'Well, it's a convenient way to get there. Otherwise you'd have to apply to Hector Neal, the owner. Don't know him personally but he's said to be rather dog-in-the-manger.'

At the age of thirty, though he looked younger, Desmond Carroll was on his first visit to Florence and the noble harmony of the city surpassed his romantic expectations. He had letters of introduction to several residents whose hospitality enhanced his appreciation of the famous sights. Among the expatriates Terence Tuckerman took him under his genial wing and regaled him with amusing local gossip, having emigrated in the 'twenties to economize when living was cheaper. His knowledge of botany compensated for his ignorance of art: he was familiar with the scientific names of plants and flowers and was proud of cultivating them in his suburban garden.

Unfortunately, the time at Desmond's disposal was limited as he had to work for a London firm of architects. He decided to join the organized tour as Terence Tuckerman suggested, and apply to Mr Neal if his garden lived up to its reputation. 'Why is it called Hercules?' he asked.

'On account of a colossus by a pupil of Michelangelo. Mr Neal removed the fig-leaf but had to replace it when he found nothing underneath. The whole place bristles with statues, not at all my type of garden. Give me the English variety, as near to nature as possible. Don't you admire my rhododendrons? I've had endless trouble with them, too much clay in the soil. Oleanders flourish here but one sees too much of them.'

Terence Tuckerman was such a chauvinist that one wondered why he had chosen to settle in Florence. His was a corner of a foreign land that remained 'forever England.'

The organized tour was exactly what Desmond had anticipated: a busload of tourists of all ages and nationalities, including rowdy brats with bubble-gum. The lady guide recited a potted history of each villa on the programme in several languages like a genteel parrot. Desmond felt sorry for her: she was obviously more civilized than her audience. Much patience and tact were required to answer the numerous queries about trees and shrubs and the symbolism of statues.

The Hercules villa came last on the list, and by the time they reached it the older tourists were so exhausted that except for an indomitable crone on crutches they stayed inside the bus. The climb up the pebbly drive bordered by tall cypresses was strenuous after trudging through half a dozen gardens on steep hillsides, ,and the villa overlooked a series of terraces with steps descending and ascending to various points of vantage.

In the late afternoon the whole garden was aglow with liquid amber light. Though the water-lilies in the fountains were already folded in slumber frogs croaked amorously from their tea-tray leaves. The guide attempted manfully to keep the group together and called stragglers to order when they drifted towards an open door to peer inside the house. In vain she tried to distract their attention from a too-pronounced Priapus which caused the girls to goggle and giggle and the bubble-gum boys to pinch them. Nor was it easy to prevent predatory fingers from plucking a gardenia or a lemon. Sticky pine-cones were collected as souvenirs.

Desmond Carroll was enchanted by the visual symphony of undulating balustrades and posturing statues against the panorama of the sparkling city below. He hoped to examine it in greater detail at leisure. In spite of Terence Tuckerman's warning he decided to appeal to its owner.

'My garden is open to tourists on Tuesdays and Thursdays from three to six p.m.,' Mr Neal replied. 'Why don't you join them? I dare not make exceptions as this would create a precedent. The crowds that come are sufficiently disturbing. They leave paper handkerchiefs, cigarette butts, tin foil, and Coca-Cola bottles in the grass. And when it rains — even the rain won't stop them — they churn up my lawns with their stiletto heels. I trust you will understand my reason for a negative reply. However, you are welcome to visit my ashram chapel if you telephone in advance.'

Desmond was not interested in the ashram chapel. Nothing daunted, he wrote to Mr Neal again but received no further token of acknowledgment. So he returned with the tourists and hid behind a colonnade till the others departed with the guide.

It was a treat to have the garden to himself. In every direction there was a delightful vista: it was full of subtle surprises. The jasmine on the upper terrace flooded the air with fragrance; cicadas chirped ever and anon in rhythmic choruses; blackbirds hopped between clumps of cut yew, and distant church bells pealed in unison with the tinkling of a neighbouring convent. Already six o'clock.

There was no more film in Desmond's camera so he sat on a stone bench to record the features that had struck him in a note-book. He was absorbed in this task when a dog started barking and a tall figure in an orange robe advanced towards him with hands joined Hindu fashion. He stood, or rather loomed, over Desmond and lisped: 'You must be Hyacinthus. I dreamt that you were coming.'

'I fear you are mistaken. I'm the Desmond Carroll who wrote for permission to visit this garden in private. In the words of a poet "I love all beauteous things, I seek and adore them", and I'm a particular lover of gardens.'

106

'Everything since Adam begins in a garden: it does not end there. I dreamt of you on a spiritual plane. You informed me that you were Hyacinthus and I'm sure that is correct. Hail, Hyacinthus, and welcome to the Soul's Gymnasium!'

His eyes, large and lustreless, scrutinized Desmond so intensely that he felt discomfited. 'You may not realise your vocation. Few of us do on this earth. Now that you are here you have much to learn and unlearn. First, you do not breathe properly. Inhale the oxygen. Let it come slowly in and out of your nostrils, like this.' Mr Neal inhaled and exhaled with an expression of rapture. 'In and out, in — out. How cool as it rushes in, how warm as it leaves the lungs! Expand and contract your chest, unbutton your shirt. Do it reverently. Enjoy the tension and relaxation. What a change from the fetid air of the city in the plain below. Proper breathing will prolong your life span. The pool of purification awaits you. Come along with me and doff your worldly garments.'

'But I've an appointment in town. I mustn't be late.'

'You have a previous appointment with me which is far more important. Come to the pool. I'll lead the way.'

'I have no bathing trunks.'

'Superfluous. The body is the temple of the Divine Ideal.'

The prospect of a cool dip after a hot day was by no means disagreeable. Why not humour the old creature for once?

While Desmond undressed Mr Neal examined him with approval. *'Mens sana in corpore sano.* Hair in the right places and proportion. Not Jewish by any chance?'

'I was brought up as an Anglican. Why do you ask?'

'I refer to the surgical detail.'

Desmond laughed shyly. 'A normal prophylactic irrespective of race or creed.'

'The integument has its merits, but let that pass; it is not essential. Your physique is promising. The mole on your right shoulder is a sign of benison. Any birthmark on the buttocks?'

'Really, Mr Neal, you make me blush.'

'I'm nothing if not straightforward. I treat you as one of the elect.'

'Then why didn't you answer my letter?'

'Your handwriting gave me no vibrations. Even when I submitted it to my pendulum it failed to respond. But that will be remedied after your initiation.'

'Please excuse me, another time. I cannot keep my girl-friend waiting.'

'Give me her name and address and I shall invite her to join us.'

'Miss Rosalie Brent. We were to meet at Doney's.'

'I'll send my car to fetch her. The matter is urgent. Your spiritual future depends on it.'

Mr Neal went off to telephone. Miss Brent was already waiting in the restaurant. 'This is all very sudden,' she replied. 'Desmond told me nothing about it. I'm not sure I ought to accept . . .'

'Everything in life is sudden — birth, copulation, and death. This is to be a rebirth and it will be a privilege for you to attend it. My Bentley will be at your disposal in fifteen minutes.'

Mr Neal padded back to the pool with a capacious bath-towel. He insisted on drying Desmond and massaging his back. Though Desmond politely protested he said it was part of the ritual before meditation.

The chapel resembled a grotto with waxworks of skulls and skeletons in lamplit alcoves. Mr Neal pressed a button and a burst of loud organ music almost made Desmond jump. Where did it come from? No instrument was visible yet the notes seemed to form great whorls of smoke in the air. Then a resonant voice recited:

'Into, above, and beyond,
From sterile dust to sperm,
From fly to pachyderm,
Ah, infinitely fond,
Enveloping each germ,
The true light shines on emperor and worm.'

'Now shut your eyes and open your soul to the light,' said Mr Neal, clasping Desmond in an adhesive embrace before he could shake himself free.

Rosalie stepped into the chapel at this moment. 'Goodness gracious, am I interrupting?' she exclaimed. 'I was told you were meditating.'

The organ boomed on. 'Hyacinthus has seen the true light,' said Mr Neal. 'He is now an initiate of the Soul's Gymnasium.'

'Is that what you call Desmond?'

'His astral name henceforth. Allow me to congratulate you on your fiancé. May the true light shine on you also!'

'We're not engaged so far as I'm aware. I'm a free-lance journalist. In fact I came to Florence for the fashion show.'

'You have entered the Soul's Gymnasium. Embrace each other.'

'We are not on such intimate terms.'

'You soon will be, Stella, for that is your astral name.' A gong resounded and Mr Neal seized their hands and led them to an open loggia where candelabra gleamed on a table laid for more guests than were visible. A juvenile butler in a sky-blue livery produced a tray of drinks in frosted goblets and Mr Neal dropped a pill into each. 'A little exercise before imbibing?' he proposed to Rosalie. Picking up a silver ball, he said: 'Try to concentrate on this symbol of pure health. I'll throw and you must catch it.'

Slowly at first, then gathering speed he tossed the ball at Rosalie who hurled it back with vigour. Mr Neal considered this a favourable omen. 'Bravo, Stella!' he shouted. 'Now you must meet my disciples.'

Tweedledum and Tweedledee, thought Desmond. They were introduced under long Indian names ending in 'nanda', but one muttered, 'I'm Ron Billings,' and the other, 'I'm Rob Nunn.' Short and stocky, they spoke in the same falsetto, preferring 'we' to the first person singular. 'Actually we are the Master's secretaries,' piped Ron. 'We are also his official readers,' Rob added. 'We read the Upanishads and the

Vedanta and Madame Blavatsky.' 'In fact there's no end to our reading. We also take down messages from the Mahatmas when we visit them on the astral plane.' Rob finished Ron's sentences so that they were indistinguishable. Desmond expected them to say 'Nohow' and 'Contrariwise', for they looked at each other and grinned like the figures in *Through the Looking-Glass*.

'Reading aloud is hard on our vocal chords,' said Ron. 'When Ron gets husky Rob takes over.'

'It's a liberal education. We have read more books in one year than in four years at the varsity.'

'The trouble with reading aloud is that we don't remember what we have read. We pay more attention to the sound than to the sense.'

'Silence!' bellowed Mr Neal as if to contradict himself. 'You must drink a toast of welcome to Hyacinthus and his fiancée.'

Rosalie repeated: 'I'm not his fiancée, get that straight. And I've no intention of marrying. I refuse to be a prey to male harassment.'

'I respect your will power,' said Mr Neal, 'though it could be applied to better purpose. I foresee that you will change your mind. You are still young and unfledged.'

'A woman's age is her secret. You should read my book *The Vulnerable Virgin*. Everybody should read it. The desired yet despised is my theme — there's a fruitful subject for your meditations.'

'Our aims are higher, but I'm glad you have a sense of mission. That will be sublimated by the Soul's Gymnasium. You and Hyacinthus will be our delegates to the outside world.'

'As a feminist I'm on my guard against male exploitations. It is time for women to take control and battle for our natural rights. That is my only mission.'

'It need not be a hindrance. A special Order for Women has been founded by the Lord Maitreya and I shouldn't be surprised if you were qualified for an abbess. But are you ready to sacrifice your soul and body to the service of the World Mother? The path of renunciation is difficult. 'No attachment to earthly things. Say to yourself, "I am lower even than a blade of grass." Dive deep into the ocean of Her divine love. Then impurities will vanish and you will be absorbed into Nirvana.'

'I'll bet it's a man's Nirvana,' she thought, but it struck her that here she had a story for the *Sunday Monitor* whose editor was interested in a symposium on religious sects. A new sect founded by a British bachelor in Florence was bound to intrigue him. Here was local colour galore: half the article was written in her mind. But she was doubtful of Mr Neal's sanity: perhaps Ron and Rob were his warders. During dinner he described his visions in esoteric language. He rambled on about the nature of ultimate reality but it all sounded hopelessly vague. His monologue was studded with Sanskrit words and phrases which added to her confusion. Shiva and Krishna, the Mahatmas and Arhats in the Himalayas — what had these to offer non-Indians, and why travel so far, even in the astral body, when the Christian Gospels offered us salvation in comprehensible language? The Great Void, of which Neal spoke with such ardour, was just a vacuum to Rosalie. There was nothing figuratively that she could get her teeth into. Materially the dinner was delicious, and she ate with a hearty appetite after her wearisome day at the fashion show, where she had concluded that it was no longer fashionable to be chic. 'Let us cease to dress for men to undress us,' she had written, 'let us dress to suit ourselves . . .'

Evidently Mr Neal was no vegetarian for he helped himself abundantly to guinea fowl, but in the middle of his dissertation his head nodded over the table and he appeared to fall asleep. He had been explaining that certain centres of the human body were awakened at various stages of evolution, and that the most significant of these was at the base of the spine. The technical term for this was *kundalini,* or serpent fire. Though a painful process, it released torrents of energy and clairvoyant power.

111

Mr Neal groaned and gasped alarmingly; he clutched the tablecloth and wriggled in his chair.

'Is he going to throw a fit?' Rosalie asked.

'Don't worry. This often happens in propitious circumstances,' Ron whispered to her. 'The ego takes leave of the physical elemental whenever the World Teacher is due to arrive from the Himalayas.'

Mr Neal rose from the table, shouting and gesticulating. 'Om, om, om,' he cried. His eyes rolled in their sockets. Ron and Rob rushed to his assistance and accompanied him with staggering footsteps to the chapel, where his groans were so blood-curdling that Rosalie said to Desmond: 'I've had enough of this, haven't you? It's high time for us to hook it while the going's good.'

Desmond beckoned to the juvenile butler for a taxi and pressed a tip into his eager hand. Ron and Rob returned in a state of euphoria. 'You're not going, are you? It is a pity to miss the climax when the Master's psychic powers are at their zenith. He becomes totally transformed by his contact with the World Teacher. If he has any message for you, we shall keep you informed. Why not join us in the pool of purification before you leave?'

Desmond and Rosalie both complained of headaches. They suspected that the pills Mr Neal had dropped into their glasses before dinner were responsible. Rosalie had been so unnerved by the experience that she decided to write it off, but not for the *Sunday Monitor,* and Desmond had no desire for another encounter with Mr Neal.

Before leaving Florence, however, Desmond wanted a last glimpse of the Hercules garden, so he decided to join another organized tour preserving his anonymity.

In the Pullman bus a talkative American youth sat beside him who, excepting an incipient beard, had the features and figure of a classical Apollo. With a naïve impulse to unbutton himself he informed Desmond that he was 'majoring in Art' at Syracuse University, New York, and that he was writing a

112

thesis on garden statuary. He was especially looking forward to the Hercules villa: was it true that it contained a masterpiece by Michelangelo? Gee, what a thrill to find a statue by the hero of *The Agony and the Ecstasy* in a private home! He confided to Desmond that he had whisked off his T-shirt and pants beside Michelangelo's *David* for a buddy to take a snapshot of them together, 'and it came out fine, Dave and I look like brothers. I guess I could do a repeat with Hercules.'

'I'll take the snapshot if you pose for it,' Desmond suggested.

'Okay, but we must watch out for the dames, they are in the majority. My name's Al Randy,' he added, 'glad to have you know me.'

Unfortunately, Al had no chance to pose beside Hercules in the nude for there were two busloads of tourists on this occasion and the lady guide kept a sharp eye on him within range of the impudent Priapus.

As before, Desmond lingered after the others had climbed into a Pullman bus. Al had the same impulse, and while he was changing his film Mr Neal walked up to him in his orange robe. From his retreat behind a box hedge Desmond heard him lisp: 'You must be Hyacinthus. I dreamt that you were coming.'

Desmond did not stay to witness further developments. He turned on his heel and ran down the cypress avenue, feeling he was pursued by vengeful statues. The iron gate on the piazza of Bellosguardo was still open. Once outside it Desmond paused to mop his forehead and recover his breath.

The trances and astral voyages of Mr Neal were as chaff to the revelation of the sunset. Surely God was in this glory of vermilion and gold. Desmond stretched forth his arms in rapture and was whistled at by an urchin on a scooter. With a sense of exaltation he sauntered towards the Porta Romana in the gathering dusk. The sheer joy of being alive, awake and alert, suffused his whole being. Could a state of higher consciousness be reached in the Great Void? He smiled at the thought of Al Randy being put through his paces at the pool of purification. The young American was sufficiently naïf to be deceived by Mr Neal's hocus-pocus — such charlatans flourished in California. But was Mr Neal a charlatan? Was he not rather his own dupe — a sophisticated simpleton with ample means to indulge his swollen ego?

The fashion show finished, Rosalie sat waiting for Desmond in Harry's Bar. 'Hail, Hyacinthus!' she greeted him.

'Hail, Mother Abbess!' he replied with a bow.

'What is your latest news from the Soul's Gymnasium?'

'I took a final peep at the garden and fled. Mr Neal has decoyed a younger Hyacinthus.'

Codicil Coda

'Don't go. I've a little surprise for you. I'm making another will and I want you to choose something personal to remember me by.'

Muriel's voice was a hoarse imploring whisper. A skeletal arm was extended from her crêpe-de-Chine dressing gown to ring for her maid. With an automatic sigh she sank back on her mound of pillows.

Jenny expostulated with her: no, she simply couldn't, the mere idea was much too painful! But Muriel had the persistence of the extremely fragile. 'I won't be with you much longer, darling, so you might afford me this trifling satisfaction. There isn't much to choose from, I'm afraid. The best things were snapped up while you were in Bermuda.'

The maid brought in a large lacquer tray covered with sparkling jewels. Jenny couldn't help exclaiming: 'Why, these would fill a shop window!'

Squirming and almost creaking with the effort, Muriel raised herself from her recumbent posture. 'Bring the tray nearer, Paquita, so that we can focus. Now, Jenny, do make up your mind. Is it to be a diamond necklace, a sapphire brooch, or the ruby earrings that belonged to the last Empress of Brazil? I'm glad to see that none of these have been booked.'

Obviously, it amused her to watch the performance she had organized so often since the doctors had consigned her to partial immobility. Nearly all her putative legatees feigned embarrassment when she announced her offer of 'some purely personal souvenir'. Confronted with the same tray of glittering gems, they could not conceal their growing excitement as they picked up a necklace or bracelet and held it tremulously against the light. Muriel prompted them to greater boldness. 'Try the necklace, dear, it will suit your complexion. Once it suited mine. Or would you fancy the emerald bracelet?'

Half her face was hidden by huge dark spectacles — so dark that one could not detect the twinkle in her eyes, which remained her liveliest feature. On the other hand Muriel could see everything: her vision was excellent. What fun it was to observe the transition from polite hesitation to naked greed as each jewel was critically examined and its beauty balanced against its commercial value. Most of her friends plumped for the diamond necklace. Some of the stones were imitations but only an expert could tell the difference. The earrings were genuine, even if they had never belonged to the Empress of Brazil. Perhaps fewer women wore them nowadays, for they seemed less popular.

What would Jenny choose? Muriel watched her with keen curiosity: her taste had always been unpredictable. Her reaction, however, was disappointing. She stood there awkwardly with a blank expression. 'Honestly, Muriel, I'd sooner leave the choice to you. You said you had a surprise for me. If I choose anything now there won't be any surprise, will there? Besides, we're about the same age. Why shouldn't you survive me?'

'Stop quibbling. I'm a hopeless wreck and you know it as well as I do. Doctor Lorimer put all the cards flat on the table: he gave me a fifty-fifty chance. And my horoscope happens to coincide. I want to be fully prepared when I go, leaving everything I value to dear friends . . .'

'Well, I think you're being morbid. Under Doctor Lorimer's care there's no reason why you shouldn't make a complete recovery.'

Muriel resented what she called 'foolish optimism'. It gave her a perverse pleasure to stir sympthy by acting as if she were iller than she felt. At the moment she was feeling buoyant: her temper rose accordingly. 'That's utter nonsense, old girl. I'm doomed.'

116

'So are we all, dear. Why be melodramatic about it?'

'You're callous. As if I enjoyed being bedridden!'

'I love staying in bed, so snug and relaxing. I'd stay there half the time if I had the chance.'

'Not if your doctor ordered it. I assure you it soon becomes monotonous. But of course you're joking. I wish I had your sense of humour.'

'Ah, but that doctor of yours is so dishy. I wouldn't mind being one of his patients.'

During this dialogue Paquita was standing disconsolately with the tray of jewels. She had done this so often that she drooped with fatigue. 'Do you require anything else, Madame?' she enquired in a plaintive tone. 'It will soon be time for your next injection.'

'What have you chosen, Jenny? For heaven's sake decide before the things go back into the safe!'

'You decide for me, darling. Concentrate on your recovery: nothing else matters. I can't see your eyes behind those awful goggles but you've better colour than you had last week. If you're waiting for an injection I'll retire.'

'Do stay. The injection can wait. Since Rodney Charlington's coronary and Letty Barlow's stroke there are several new gaps in my codicil. I want you to help me fill them. Come on, Jenny, be a sport! You've done me many a good turn in the past, please do me this final favour!'

'Let me have one of your portraits. You've plenty to spare...' Jenny glanced at the paintings crowding every wall. Realistic, surrealistic, even abstract, one would never guess that they were all intended to portray Muriel. Even when the realists had attempted flattery it was evident that the model had fallen short of beauty. In each there was one disagreeable feature: the eyes were hard, the mouth supercilious or sullen, and there was a general air of defiant contempt.

Muriel had been determined to preside over every room in effigy, if not in flesh and blood. The flesh had withered and the blood had thinned: physically she had become very remote from these varied patterns of colour. 'Van Dongen, Marie Laurencin, Foujita — who haven't you posed for in your time? I think I prefer the Marie Laurencin,' said Jenny. 'It's as chic as when she painted it.'

'There's also a Picasso. I've been responsible for some of the supreme examples of modern art. And behind each portrait is a love affair. Sorry, Jenny, I've promised the whole lot to Hugo Pine's museum. When I vanish these will illustrate a summit of civilization. I all but breathe in them.'

'I'd be just as happy with a photograph. The Cecil Beaton for instance. Yes, I'd rather have that. He has caught your charisma . . .'

'It's a poor substitute for a diamond necklace, which is what I hoped you would choose. I'll have to consider it.'

'Couldn't I take it along with me?'

'We were discussing bequests, dear. Actually I don't want to part with it — not just yet. It reminds me of what I used to be. I peep at it when I'm low and it bucks me up.'

'Forgive me. I never dreamt you'd miss it.' Indeed, Muriel was far too possessive to part with anything during her lifetime, or what remained of it.

A whiff of iodoform preceded the entry of a nurse with Paquita — this time with a medicine trolley. Jenny tactfully averted her gaze. Blowing Muriel a kiss, she said: 'I really must be off. I'll look in again tomorrow.'

'Please stay for supper. Quentin will mix you a drink in the drawing-room.'

'Alas, I'm already engaged.'

'Don't desert a dying pal. Since Bertie caught influenza I've been terribly lonely.'

'But you still have Quentin with you.'

'Quentin is hardly what I call company. Be an angel and stay!'

While Paquita and the nurse were preparing Muriel for her injection Jenny tiptoed out of the room. In the corridor lined with more portraits she stopped before a pastel of Muriel's

118

famous mother. Lady Lavinia's beauty had a classical perfection which stood apart, like a luminous idea among platitudes. Curious that her favourite daughter had inherited no vestige of that legendary charm. Muriel owed everything to her mother except her looks. Though she had managed to create an independent image by dabbling in the arts she had never emancipated herself from Lady Lavinia's aura. Historically her mother had outlived her.

While Jenny was admiring the pastel a sudden scream made her jump. She fled to the drawing-room where Quentin was dispensing hospitality to a group of regulars. In Bertie's absence he had the run of the house. How this epicene creature had come into Muriel's life remained as mysterious as his origins. Once there he had dug himself in. She referred to him as her *bonne à tout faire,* and indeed he was ready to do anything to oblige her and her guests so long as they did not poach on his preserves, which had become more extensive since Muriel's decline. He had his own trendy flat on an upper floor. Old Bertie had precedence, but Bertie had been her official paramour: at least he still assumed the role in public.

For a woman so totally self-absorbed Muriel had an astonishing number of sycophantic slaves. She treated them despotically, sending them on capricious errands and scolding them like children for any incompetence. Eager to be in at the death, which might happen any moment, the most assiduous haunted her house daily. Ever expectant, yet loathing each other, they occupied various 'Louis-Louis' chairs near the table where Quentin was juggling with an Art Deco cocktail shaker while some played bridge in a corner.

Quentin bent over to kiss Jenny's hand in continental fashion. 'What may I pour your ladyship?' he asked with unction.

'Oh, anything strong. I was depressed by Muriel's condition. She's excessively concerned about that will of hers. And her scream unnerved me.'

'She always screams at the sight of a needle. You should have seen her yesterday. We had a nasty scare. She was treated with a blood transfusion.'

'She begged me to stay for supper. I'm afraid I can't.'

'Please do. It would be an act of charity to me as well as to her. She's so tired of' (he lowered his voice) 'the usual pack of vultures.'

The latter consisted of distant cousins and a few ambassadors' widows. They wore the same vaguely distraught expression.

'I suppose Jenny's been shown the crown jewels,' said Pamela Bodkin with a twitch.

'Surely she must have seen them before. Poor Muriel's memory has been fading rapidly. She has asked me to choose from the same tray half a dozen times. One should pretend to join her little game. It gives her a kick to whet one's appetite.'

'I wonder how often she has touched up her will in the last year.'

'Every day I expect, and every night. What else has she to do?'

'I must say she looks pretty ghastly. It makes one shudder. So diaphanous!'

'I thought she seemed somewhat livelier. She slapped her nurse and threw a pillow at Quentin. That's surely a sign of improvement.'

'The patience of Quentin! It's amazing what he puts up with.'

'*Et pour cause.* Have you seen his new Mercedes?'

'I confess I've had a surfeit of tantrums, but one can't help commiserating. Her martyrdom seems endless.'

'Jenny's arrived late on the scene. I'll bet you she's after the diamond necklace.'

'Too many are. She doesn't stand a chance. Blood runs thicker than water. I'm only a second cousin but there are several nieces who deserve priority.'

'If I were Muriel I'd swallow an overdose. I believe it's the heart this time and no wonder. It's been under a heavy strain.'

'I should have thought it was the liver. How she used to gourmandize! Remember when we called her the foie-gras fiend? I brought her some but she asked me to exchange it for Persian caviare. Have you any idea what's for supper?'

'The usual sole boiled in milk, followed by caramel custard I expect . . .'

'Then I'll excuse myself from regimental duties. I'm pining for a juicy steak.'

So the slaves chatted in undertones while Quentin refilled their glasses. They were invariably thirstier when drinks were 'on the house'. Since nobody could smoke in Muriel's presence they lit one cigarette after another from her Fabergé boxes of Turkish and Virginian tobacco. Quentin was a lavish host in Muriel's absence. 'Full marks to you for hospitality!' said Pamela. 'I'll pop in again tomorrow. Our poor invalid dreads being left alone with her thoughts.'

'I don't agree,' said Jenny. 'Apart from her will — or wills — she's dictating her autobiography.'

'Well, she's had a colourful past. That should be some consolation.'

A temple gong resounded and Muriel, supported by her butler on one side and Paquita on the other, tottered and swayed across the Aubusson carpet towards the central divan. Swathed in clouds of snowy chiffon, it was a spectral apparition. The visitors were hushed in awe. 'How ethereal!' Pamela murmured. Muriel vouchsafed no sign of recognition. A nurse followed her with a panoply of shawls, cushions and hot water bottles. Very gently she was lifted and lowered onto the long divan. Paquita then handed her a mirror in which she examined her face. After powdering her nose and applying lipstick rather crookedly she pointed towards the bucket of champagne beside her. The butler filled her glass and while she sipped it her guests advanced in single file to greet her.

'I hope Quentin has done the honours: that's what he's there for. Jenny will be staying for supper. The rest of you may go. Thank you for being so kind and be sure I won't forget it.'

Again Jenny tried to excuse herself. 'Gervase is waiting for me and I'm already late. Forgive me, darling, but I haven't the heart to chuck him. He flies back to Bermuda tomorrow.'

'Let him, he's fit as a fiddle. He'll be flying round the world when I'm pushing up the daisies.'

This was sheer blackmail, but Jenny had to surrender when Muriel burst into tears. The others were none too sorry to retire. Quentin seldom got an evening off duty. 'I'm a bird of paradise in a gilded cage,' he remarked, forgetting it was the gilt that kept him there.

A small dinner table was wheeled up to the divan. The champagne bucket was within easy reach of Muriel's arm, and she continued to replenish her glass without spilling it or offering some to Jenny, who had no desire for the wine but wished she would speak louder. Her voice scarcely rose above a whisper as she reverted to the subject of her bequests and the sensational memoirs she was frantically dictating between recoveries and relapses.

'You must help me to find a good title. Provisionally I'm calling it *Muriel on Muriel, faute de mieux*. Pamela suggested *Lady Lavinia's Daughter,* which sounds like a Victorian novel. Though I worshipped my mamma I want to stand on my own — no borrowed plumes. My agent is negotiating for the serial rights . . .'

Her speech became blurred and breathless as the wine went to her head. It was a curious monologue about her Plantagenet ancestors, followed by Jacobites and Hanoverians. The Jacobites became confused with Jacobins, the beddings with weddings, bastards with elopements and royal mistresses. Actually she seemed to be talking to herself rather than to Jenny, inventing her private mythology. 'It was my vocation to become a legend,' she declared.

As Muriel rambled on and on Jenny repented that she had sacrificed an evening with Gervase for this. What a genius for self-deceit, she reflected. After coffee was served the butler entered with a telegram on a silver salver. 'Please open it for me, darling. I've a phobia for telegrams nowadays.'

122

Jenny stared at its contents in dismay. She feared its effect on Muriel at this juncture.

'For heaven's sake, read it aloud. Let's hear the worst.'

'Bad news, I'm afraid. Dulcie and Aileen both killed in an aircrash.'

'Oh dear, how terribly tiresome. I'll have to change my codicil again. I was leaving Dulcie my sapphire parure and Aileen my jade pendant — the one I bought from the Empress Dowager's chief eunuch. Now, Jenny, I shall never forgive you unless you agree to take the sapphire parure.'

But Jenny could not answer, for she fell over the table in a dead faint. Paquita helped to revive her with smelling salts and brandy, but when she attempted to walk she stumbled and would have fallen again had Paquita not caught her. 'Can't think what's come over me,' she muttered. 'I feel like death.' Her eyes stared vacantly from a blotchy face and her mouth was twisted on one side. The words she uttered incessantly became incomprehensible. There could be no doubt that this was serious. Muriel was unable to make any sense out of her convulsive mouthings. 'Pull yourself together, darling,' she repeated to deaf ears. Poor Jenny seemed far gone. Paquita had a struggle to keep her quiet while an ambulance was sent for. Unfortunately, the trained nurse had flounced off in a rage since Muriel had slapped her again and broken her spectacles. Time dragged on leaden feet till the ambulance arrived and Jenny was carried into it.

Muriel had drained a whole bottle of champagne in the meantime. One after another, she mused, her best friends had let her down. Jenny was the last straw. Hang the lot of them! After all the care she had lavished on her legacies they had made her appear a legacy-hunter in reverse. Though she had hunted them with necklaces, bracelets and brooches, the bag, her final codicil, was empty. Paquita was the one and only person she could count on. She had stuck to her through thick and thin for she forgot how many years. Come to think of it — why had it never occurred to her before? — Muriel ought to make some provision for her in her will. But in which of her numerous wills?

II

Muriel's retinue of visitors had dwindled to a mere trickle. At least six months had elapsed since the last exhibition of her jewels. The dictation of her autobiography, however, served as a tonic distraction. But her memory was weaker than her imagination: she embroidered rococo variations on the same incidents and episodes, much to the bewilderment of Miss Foxton, her patient secretary.

Between them stood a table of medicines and toilet requisites dominated by the silver-framed photograph of Muriel as a débutante. This she would contemplate now and then with an air of pensive piety, as if it were the image of her patron saint. As usual she could not bear too much light. In the penumbra of her bedroom she could nourish the illusion that she was beautiful. But it was a strain on Miss Foxton's eyesight, for she could hardly see the pad on which she was jotting down Muriel's reminiscences in shorthand. The room reeked of ether and iodoform which even the mass of tuberoses could not camouflage.

Miss Foxton was reconciled to these exacting sessions by the refreshment of gin and tonic. Gin fortified her against the intermittent tantrums of her employer, who scolded her for inattention when she spoke in a mumbled whisper. At first the secretary had the courage to warn her when she repeated the same anecdote.

'Never mind,' said Muriel crossly. 'I'll select the best version later. Don't ever stop me during my flights of inspiration! Ours was always a very grand family,' she dictated, 'ever since — oh dear, I forget our precise connection with Charlemagne. I'll have to look it up. I'm not ashamed, as so many are these radical chic days, of being born with a golden spoon in my mouth. (Remove that mirror. I don't want to see myself as I am but as I used to be.) My father was only the younger son of a younger son, but he was directly descended from an unbroken line of Saxon kings and Norman crusaders. My mother was the granddaughter of a Russian Grand Duchess. However, this isn't their biography, it is mine and something to be proud of. Unlike the majority of society girls, as they used to be called, I have made the most of my creative gifts and seen the rosiest dreams of my youth come true. Love — I'm bound to confess that I have had rather more than my fair share of it. Even in the cradle my cheeks were tickled by a royal moustache. I gurgled with delight, and the smell of his special eau-de-Cologne has remained with me ever since; the sound of H.R.H.'s hearty guffaw still rings in my ears. Yes, I let myself go at a very tender age. My wet-nurse once found me blowing kisses to the sun. Later on I definitely preferred the moon. The gallant astronauts have not affected this preference. While I think of the moon with rapture, I never went in for sun-bathing, in fact I'm sure it is harmful.

'No doubt I was a naughty child but I have always maintained that naughtiness in children is a proof of vitality. Of course I was hopelessly spoiled as little girls should be, especially when they're made of sugar and spice and all that's nice. At home we were given plover's eggs for breakfast . . .'

Plover's eggs led to a discursion about the copious meals of her youth, their rich ingredients and often fatal consequences, such as the premature demise of good King Edward. And so she rambled on until she dropped asleep with her mouth open. After a doze she would waken and continue: 'As I was saying...'

There came a day when Muriel was no longer in the mood for dictation. *'A quoi bon?'* she sighed.

'What's that, ma'am? Sorry, I don't get it.'

'Muttering to myself — a sign of senility. It suddenly struck me, who am I doing this for? I must be doing it for somebody, but for whom? Blest if I know.'

125

'For eternity,' said Miss Foxton brightly.

'A fig for eternity! I want my memoirs to be read while I'm alive, or half alive. Who on earth will care to read me? A has-been, that's what I am.'

'Personally I'm enjoying it and I have a fair claim to represent the common reader. All my friends and neighbours are bound to lap it up. We'll have to revise the typescript of course. It will look even better in print. And the illustrations will be an extra attraction.'

'It has been a futile form of self-indulgence. Wallowing in worldly vanities when I should have been thinking of my soul. I've been terribly earthbound. Music might help to exalt me but I'm sick of the radio. As I can't accommodate an orchestra I'll have to hire a quartet. Beethoven will lend me the wings I need to fly with.'

'Your autobiography is beginning to take shape. Now that we've reached your first love affair it would be a shame to stop.'

'Better chuck it. You have made me realize how tired I am of myself. Don't you ever get tired of yourself, Miss Foxton?'

'I'm too busy earning my living to give it a thought.'

'Don't you regret not having little ones?'

'I beg your pardon?'

'I mean children to hug and kiss — the patter of little feet.'

Miss Foxton tittered. 'I'm not yet out of the running. You should tell us about *your* little ones. That's what your women readers want to hear, me included.'

Muriel disregarded this indiscreet suggestion. She tugged furiously at her bell-rope and flung the bed-pan at her secretary, who retreated in panic towards the door. Paquita rushed in with an alarmed expression, for the bell-rope was only used in emergencies. Her eyes flashing, Muriel pointed at the retreating figure.

'Get rid of that insolent baggage!' she shrilled.

Miss Foxton tripped over the bed-pan with a clatter and slammed the door. Soon the butler appeared with restorative champagne. He poured it with a furtive smile. Still trembling

126

from her recent outburst, Muriel spilled half her glass and dabbed some behind her ears for luck. 'Ah, that's the best blood transfusion!' she murmured, and swallowed several glasses in succession. Like a delicious sap the wine flowed upward and flushed her waxen cheeks. She asked for her address-book and turned its pages. The names of her chief legatees had been crossed out. She began to cross out more and half way through shut the book with an exasperated snap. Squeamish Beamish, Guy Digmore, Julia Latrobe, Lettice Rigby, Percival Sackbut — dead every one of them. The last to go was poor Jenny. She felt guilty for not giving her the photograph she wanted... Hermione, Pamela, Charlotte had gone before. Quentin had married an alcoholic widow and sailed off to the Caribbean in her yacht.

Muriel's coterie had been disbanded and she had nobody to grumble to except Paquita. Her own existence, such as it was, seemed to have been prolonged by illness, the *mauvaise santé de fer*. That cramping pain was shooting up her shoulder. Her will-power fought it: no morphine yet, however intense the aching of her bones.

'Bring me the trinkets, Paquita,' she pleaded. Before her next injection she must remove the labels of dead friends. To whom should she bequeath them? Their intrinsic value — but her head was too dizzy for calculation — must have tripled in all these years. The emerald and diamond clasp of her pearl necklace alone was said to exceed the value of the pearls, which had been deflated by Japanese 'culture' products. She had not worn it for ages — not since the costume ball in Venice when she had represented Catherine the Great surrounded by lusty Cossacks.

What a dazzling entry she had made in that palace on the Grand Canal! More Cleopatra than Catherine, it was remarked, as she advanced to the fanfare of an orchestra with all the lights concentrated on her majestic figure. Never had she felt so completely identified with the queen of her imagination. Smiling graciously she had stood beside the host, a stocky Mexican who had puffed himself up in high buskins and vast periwig to personate the Sun King. So many impersonations on that night, most of them comically incongruous. Only Muriel had borne a resemblance to the role she had selected. Anyone could dress up, but how few could play the part with dignity. Mary Stuart, for instance, with a long cigarette holder, and the Roman emperors who did not know what to do with their hands and feet, betraying by every gesture that they belonged to the twentieth century. The blaze of Venetian chandeliers accentuated their anachronisms, and the heat had become so oppressive that many guests slipped out into the piazza behind the palace where an accordion seemed to fan a cooling breeze. These quenched their thirst in a neighbouring café and their costumes were applauded vociferously by groups of gondoliers. Soon couples were dancing merrily on the pavement. The Cossacks twirled with each other and Muriel danced with an enterprising young gondolier. He had kissed her hand like a courtier, and before the night was over he had made passionate love to her in his gondola. His sobs of joy had flattered her more than speeches. She tingled at the recollection of this fugitive affair. It had been her last voluptuous fling. Since then she had collected accidents and operations. At present she would not care to be seen by her former lovers, for her face was ravaged beyond the aid of cosmetics and her brittle bones seemed to burst through her skin.

While she was ruminating in a cerebral hothouse of tangled growths, Paquita appeared with several trays of jewels. Muriel told her to put them on the counterpane. One by one she removed the labels from bracelets and brooches and dusted them with cotton wool. The ruby and diamond bracelet she slipped over one minute wrist, the emerald bracelet over the other; she covered her bodice with a breastplate of brooches and pearl pendants and crammed every finger with rings, two or three to each finger, so loose that they dangled in circles against each other. The Grand Duchess's pearl and diamond tiara was adjusted to her fluffy wig and the sapphire ear-clips concealed her flabby lobes. Her skinny neck, shoulders and arms were entirely encrusted in the most precious of cut and cabochon stones.

Paquita stood gaping and gasping in astonishment as jewel after jewel was transferred from each tray to Muriel's fragile anatomy. Accoutred like a barbaric idol, Muriel lay back on her pillows, panting from the effort of her transformation. Recovering breath, she asked for her hand-mirror. At first she was appalled by the reflection of her face as she searched for remnants of the beauty she had lost. 'This harridan can't possibly be me,' she thought. All the same it was rather wonderful. Her enlarged feverish eyes still outshone the tiara in her wig. Nobody could deny that the wreck of her features amid the glitter of jewels was intensely dramatic. She was reminded of Mallarmé's *Hérodiade*. 'Yes, it is for myself, deserted, that I flower!' She quoted not ineptly.

Her life had been a gradually expiring Carnival but it had not yet expired. She hoped it would flicker out gently and discreetly . . . The cramping pains had increased. While Paquita's back was turned she gave herself a quick jab with the morphine she kept handy. Though the weight of her jewels was uncomfortable the relief was instantaneous. No moon shone into her room, yet she had the sensation of being flooded with moonlight, reclining on fleecy clouds, wafted heavenwards by the strong scent of tuberoses. The wrinkles left her face; her lips, which usually drooped with discontent, were smiling serenely. 'How beautiful!' exclaimed Paquita.

Yes, Muriel made a beautiful corpse.

Muriel died intestate. No draft of any will could be found among her papers, the accumulation of over seventy years. She left voluminous diaries which contained a few cryptic references to bequests but these had no legal value. Her funeral was private and Paquita was the only mourner. Brief obituaries referred to Muriel as Lady Lavinia's daughter, who had been painted by many artists of conflicting tendencies

129

between the two world wars. Her interesting collection would probably be sold at auction. This included some highly important jewellery.

A Phantom Botticelli

Everybody agreed that the *pièce de résistance* of the historic Palazzo Lapi was its so-called refectory. Fifteenth-century wedding chests adorned with mythological scenes by Tuscan artists whose names are only known to a few scholars like Sir John Pope-Hennessy lined the lower part of the walls; above them hung early panels of tempera and gold in a subtle crescendo of colour towards a representation of the Last Supper by a close disciple of Giotto. Maiolica vases of the same period glowed on the carved sideboards of oak and walnut, museum pieces all.

Martin Wilmer had devoted decades of fastidious selection and rejection to its arrangement, with a result that was sumptuous yet austere. He felt assured that he had achieved aesthetic perfection within this cloistered area. Nothing could be added or subtracted without spoiling its harmony. *'Ici je bois du lait,'* he remarked, almost purring like a cat before a dish of cream. The cliché-reaction of visitors was 'absolutely breathtaking!'

It was therefore a shock when his crony Professor Norbert Pfister informed him that the walls of this room had been frescoed by Botticelli in 1484. An industrious archivist, the Professor quoted documentary evidence to prove his dramatic assertion. He was intensely exhilarated by his discovery and he expected Martin to share his elation. 'To think that a masterpiece has been hiding here all these centuries!' he exclaimed. 'Fortunately there has been immense progress in the technique of restoration since Botticelli's frescoes in the Villa Lemmi were sold to the Louvre. Having been protected by layers of plaster indoors, these are probably in mint condition. Don't you long to set eyes on them? I can hardly wait!'

Martin listened glumly to the Professor's anticipatory raptures. Apparently he was expected to turn his precious refectory topsy-turvy and start scraping its walls at once. Pfister lectured him as if it were his moral duty to art, to history, to culture. Martin shuddered at such a prospect. 'Is not this room a consummate work of art? Could any fresco improve it, however fine? I should have to remove the furniture and all the pictures I have chosen with such care. You are asking me to take a terrible risk.'

'Botticelli is worth every risk. Another Venus may rise in splendour from this plaster. What are these wooden derivatives of Giotto compared to the athletic grace of the sublime Sandro?' He snapped his fingers at the Primitive Madonnas and Saints around him.

Hitherto Martin had enjoyed the Professor's company and taken an interest in his researches, which had supplied exact dates for several of his pictures. Pfister was also an expert on Tuscan wines and cooking. He could distinguish between the vintages of Chianti, 'the Cock' and 'the Cherub', and he had introduced Martin to many a savoury dish. Together they had made excursions to rustic eating houses for the sake of some speciality which the Professor ascribed to Etruscan origin. Not only had they culinary predilections in common but also a penchant for cemeteries, where they went for leisurely walks, stopping ever and anon before a tombstone to translate an epitaph and ponder on the character of the mortal beneath it. Martin was tall and angular with a monocle, the Professor short and tubby with bifocal lenses on the tip of his nose; the former spruce, the latter dishevelled: they formed an incongruous couple among the florid funerary sculpture. The old English cemetery where Mrs Browning and Landor were buried was their favourite resort, though Martin could not agree with Landor's line, 'Nature I loved, and next to nature art', for he preferred art to nature at all times.

132

They had first met at one of Miss Prudence Royle's Thursday At Homes, where the hostess dispensed Ceylon tea and Scotch scones to a polyglot circle of dilettanti, and Martin had been impressed by the Professor's erudition. He had collaborated with Miss Royle on a study of the Florentine *Arti*, or Trade-guilds. 'I supplied the facts and Miss Royle the local colour,' he remarked. 'Miss Royle is a great manipulator of atmosphere.'

A devotee of Nietzsche, Pfister often quoted as his motto: 'The sense for fact, the last and most valuable of all senses.' His own sense for fact was gratified in archives wherever he happened to be. A natural instinct guided him to the fact he wanted, and to others which cropped up as a bonus, as in this instance.

Martin was so disconcerted by the Professor's last discovery and so vexed by his presumption that he no longer saw him as a friend but as an agent of the devil. 'I'll have to think it over,' he murmured. 'I restored this palace room by room after it had been desecrated by previous owners, and my most beautiful room is this refectory. Yes, I'll have to think it over. We shall see.'

'I hope we shall see another *Primavera*. You should have X-rays taken as soon as possible.'

The Professor was disappointed by Martin's lack of response. He suspected that his love of art, like that of many collectors, was restricted to his private possessions, while Martin detected self-promotion behind the Professor's zeal. Headlines in the newspapers; a spate of articles in academic journals; interviews allowing him to parade his pedantry — were evidently flickering through his mind. After the penumbra of archives he looked forward to a sunbath of publicity. It was Professor Pfister rather than Botticelli who would capture the attention of the media.

The Professor chuckled and rubbed his hands while Martin gazed at his Madonnas with a silent prayer to save his sanctum from depredation. 'The document described this room without any shadow of doubt,' the Professor insisted, 'and X-rays will help us to unveil the masterpiece.'

Like a cancer, thought Martin, escorting him to the door. 'Damn and blast the Nosy Parker!' he shouted as soon as the Professor left him. He stepped into his open courtyard to cool his temper. It was an ethereal blue evening and the stars were glimmering overhead. The slender columns of *pietra serena* evoked an Annunciation by Fra Angelico, but what a difference between the Professor and the angel Gabriel! Yet the Professor fancied that he had brought glad tidings.

Now an elderly bachelor of ample means, Martin Wilmer had bought the Palazzo Lapi at the turn of the century when he had begun to collect paintings by the followers of Giotto. The stylistic variations between these were scarcely perceptible to an untutored eye, but by living with them and comparing them with their contemporaries in churches and galleries Martin could attribute them to definite personalities of the Trecento. The simple piety of these early masters, their innocent vision and purity of colour, never ceased to enchant him. Nearly all his pictures had golden backgrounds which glowed like sunsets against his cream-coloured walls. Martin enjoyed discussing their merits with art historians whose conflicting opinions provided him with the entertainment that others found in the theatre. Even his creature comforts were sacrificed to his artefacts. Since central heating caused panels to split and paint to crackle he kept the temperature low. In winter the house was so frigid that Martin wore his heavy overcoat indoors.

Owing to the multitude of Madonnas his servants imagined that he was deeply religious, but his religion was confined to his collection: he spent whole mornings in churches for the sake of their altarpieces and frescoes rather than for that of his soul. Unless the music were Gregorian he seldom attended High Mass.

'Preciosity, thy name is Martin Wilmer!' his friend Prudence Royle used to say. His ultra-refinement cut him off from less sophisticated pleasures: perhaps it was perversely enjoyable not to enjoy. Puccini was as anathema as Wagner to him, and he could only approve of Beethoven's last Quartets. He cared less for Botticelli than for Taddeo Gaddi.

To resist Professor Pfister's importunity Martin refused to answer the telephone and paid no attention to his urgent notes. But the disciple of Nietzsche bore in mind his master's definition of happiness: 'the feeling that power increases, that a resistance is overcome.' He had a stubborn will, and he reported his discovery to the ministry of arts with a plea for immediate action. But the ways of bureaucracy are slow even in Italy where it is endemic, and many weeks passed before Martin was obliged to receive an official visit from Dr Cipollini, the regional director. He was accompanied by Professor Pfister, who must have realized that he was not *persona grata*, yet he behaved as if he were Martin's landlord 'Dr Cipollini is so cruelly overworked that it is not easy to coax him away from his office,' he said. 'I am delighted by this opportunity to show him the jewels of your collection and the hall which was formerly frescoed by Botticelli. Dr Cipollini is a leading authority on the sublime Sandro.'

'You do me too much honour, dear Professor. I have published one or two trifles of which I need not be ashamed, little aids to the metaphysical understanding of the master in relation to the social structure of Florence during the second half of the fifteenth century, with particular emphasis on the iconography of his cosmological allegories.'

'So you see he has come to the right place. Even if the subject of the fresco is as complicated as the *Calumny of Apelles*, Dr Cipollini will be able to explain it.'

'Its existence depends on a superannuated inventory. I consider it a doubtful ·speculation. This palace has often changed hands since the fifteenth century, but surely they would have preserved an important work of art?'

'Tastes change, especially in interior decoration. Botticelli would have seemed old-fashioned in the eighteenth century.

Be that as it may, he belongs to our national heritage. In my official capacity it will be my duty to make a scientific investigation. I hope you appreciate our concern in this project, inspired by our learned friend's discovery in the archives.' Dr Cipollini bowed to the Professor with a deferential smile.

Martin protested: 'But this house is mine and possession is nine points of the law. What if I refuse to allow the spoliation of my refectory?'

'In the matter of recovering a lost Botticelli you are merely a trustee. You will receive a formal application to let us proceed with the operation. You disregard it at your peril.'

'Who will pay for it? At a conservative estimate it will cost millions. I could never afford the expense.'

'You need not worry. The government will grant a special subsidy.'

'And if there's a hitch,' the Professor added, 'I know an art-loving Croesus who will subscribe for the glory of it. No problem, Mr Wilmer. Just leave it to Dr Cipollini and relax. This will be a privilege for all of us, to witness the rebirth of a masterpiece.'

In due course Martin received a peremptory demand from the ministry, couched like a veiled menace. He was to afford Dr Cipollini every facility for uncovering the fresco which he held on trust for the nation. Martin consulted his lawyer, who told him candidly that he had no chance of winning a case against a government official. Dr Cipollini had influence in high places and it was advisable to make concessions, however disagreeable, for he could be a dangerous enemy if thwarted. 'As an art collector you may require his services — a permission for an export licence for instance. It is worth your while to oblige him.'

'Is he bribable? I'd pay anything to save my refectory.'

'Fie, Mr Wilmer. Dr Cipollini is what you call a VIP.'

'Supposing I offered him one of my *fondi oro* with a hint to leave my refectory alone? After all, it is the pride of my palace.'

136

'Times have changed. Dr Cipollini is a prominent official. And thanks to Professor Pfister it has been widely reported that it contains a fresco by Botticelli.'

'That is by no means certain. It has yet to be proved.'

'Well, Dr Cipollini is determined to prove it. For him it is a matter of personal prestige. No, Mr Wilmer, your best policy under the circumstances is a diplomatic compromise. That should not be difficult for an Englishman.'

'The concession would be one-sided. For me it is heartrending.'

Martin was forced to surrender. Dr Cipollini turned up with a lorry full of instruments and a squadron of technicians. Martin stood impotently by while they invaded his refectory, rolled up the carpets, unhooked the paintings, and filled the air with garlic and the fumes of tobacco, scattering their chattels on his furniture. Once inside they treated it as their domain. Martin fled to barricade himself in the rest of the building.

A large van arrived with ladders which were propped against the walls, since the infra-red rays had shown, to a chorus of excitement, that a fresco lay hidden under the plaster. Professor Pfister strutted about joking with the workmen. He had brought a flask of Chianti to toast their success. First they decided to scrape a section of the wall where a trace of colour had been detected by the powerful lens. The Professor was bursting with optimism. *'Bravi, c'e l'abbiamo già trovato!'* he exclaimed, gleefully clapping his hands.

After several days of chiselling some bearded figures emerged. 'Why, it's Garibaldi's landing at Marsala!' Dr Cipollini observed.

'No, there is also an image of the *Re Galantuomo*.'

'Evviva Garibaldi! Botticelli couldn't have painted a better likeness,' said the chief technician.

After the surface patches had been removed the plaster flaked off easily. Soon a garish relic of the Risorgimento came to light. Together with Garibaldi and Victor Emmanuel a company of Red-shirts were being fêted by buxom wenches with baskets of fruit and garlands of flowers. Everybody but the Professor burst out laughing. 'We shall have to dig deeper,' he said sadly. But the infra-red rays failed to detect any under-painting. 'Nevertheless we must persevere.'

'It would be a pity to damage this historic record,' said Dr Cipollini. 'It might have been painted by Fattori, a most estimable artist of the period.'

In a corner the artist's name could be deciphered: *Papucci pinxit*. The omniscient Professor remembered that Papucci's portrait of Mrs Light had been mentioned by Henry James in *Roderick Hudson*. 'Well, if it's not by Botticelli it's a grand period piece,' said Dr Cipollini by way of consolation.

'Period piece, period,' snapped the discouraged Professor. 'I see nothing grand about it. The colours are vulgar and the composition crude, like an illustration to a popular magazine.'

'I was thinking of the subject,' said Dr Cipollini. 'For us Italians, that is grand.'

Since nothing but bricks and mortar was visible after further scraping Dr Cipollini decided to stop work. Without any apology to Martin he and his myrmidons packed up and withdrew, leaving the refectory like an abandoned carpenter's shop, coated with dust, cigarette butts, and chips of plaster. Professor Pfister doggedly returned to the archives to pursue his researches. As Martin had pointed out, his palace had had many proprietors since the Quattrocento: there were other houses belonging to the Lapi with which it might have been confused. Pfister examined the parchment registers of property in the neighbourhood and inspected their sites, now converted into offices and apartments. Eventually he came to the conclusion that the Palazzo Lapi containing Botticelli's handiwork had been demolished when Florence became the capital of Italy.

Martin Wilmer had been sacrificed to a case of mistaken identity and he received no compensation. Unfortunately, the journalists who had been prompted by Pfister to publish articles about his discovery brought Martin's collection into the dreaded limelight. This acted as a boomerang when the putative Botticelli turned into a Papucci. The flying leap from the Renaissance to the Risorgimento provoked much sarcasm at the Professor's expense. In revenge Martin decided to hold a reception in the Papucci fresco's honour. He intended to camouflage the walls after the party, but his refectory would never be the same. Printed invitations were issued 'to celebrate Professor Norbert Pfister's discovery' but the Professor was excluded from the list of guests. The journalists brought their attendant photographers; a band was engaged to play Mameli's anthem; and Prudence Royle, who had written an extravaganza about the Brownings in Florence, was prevailed upon to recite *Casa Guidi Windows*. Members of the Society for Risorgimento Studies considered that the fresco was worthy of preservation but Martin had no desire to preserve it in his house. As Dr Cipollini reminded him that a law prohibited its destruction he offered it to the museum of modern art on condition that it was detached from his walls. Dr Cipollini regretted his ministry lacked funds for so expensive an enterprise: the patriotic pageant would have to remain *in situ*. Martin's only solution was to conceal it under movable canvas.

The lurid transformation of his refectory gave Martin a nervous breakdown which the sequel aggravated. One morning he woke up to find that ten of his most valuable Madonnas had vanished. He rang for his butler and pointed to the empty spaces with a trembling hand. The butler was stunned when, after a few minutes, he understood what had happened. A back door was wide open: evidently that was where the burglars had decamped with the booty. As it was Sunday the butler presumed that the maids had left it open on their way to church. Here and there an empty frame was lying on the floor near the butler's quarters.

'Did you hear nothing? Did not the watchdog bark?'

'I could only hear thunder. The dog is sick,' he replied. 'He vomited on the carpet.'

Martin felt as sick as the dog while he gazed at the gaps

where his masterpieces had hung. He summoned the police, who spent the rest of the morning searching for clues — a broken grille and window, a discarded step-ladder, but no fingerprints. The staff were interrogated as a formality though Martin assured the police that they were above suspicion. His tentative suspects were the workmen who had scraped the walls for Dr Cipollini; one of the journalists brought by Professor Pfister might also have had a finger in the pie. He produced photographs of his stolen paintings and gave the police Professor Pfister's address with a recommendation to ransack his premises.

When accounts of the robbery appeared in the newspapers strangers telephoned that they had seen the stolen paintings and were ready to disclose their whereabouts for a suitable reward. Exorbitant sums were mentioned — far more than Martin had paid for the pictures, which he had not been able to insure. A clairvoyant promised to find them if he paid her earnest-money, but as soon as he procured a tape-recorder the mysterious voices were silent. He who had shunned publicity was pointed out as the English art collector who had been robbed. He was asked continually, 'What is the latest news? Have any of your pictures turned up?' By now they were probably hidden in the bowels of a bank.

To protect the rest of his collection he installed a complicated alarm system, the disadvantage of which was that it behaved like an hysterical woman, sending forth ear-splitting screams for no apparent reason at inconvenient hours. The exaggerated sensibility of this apparatus affected Martin with a twitch beyond his control. The automatic winking of an eye was often misinterpreted by street passengers, who thought he was making passes at them. In fact he was profoundly disgusted with people and became a semi-recluse. Prudence Royle admonished him: 'Pull up your socks, love. Remember you're a true blue Briton. Never say die!' Nevertheless, part of him had died with the loss of his pictures and the destruction of his refectory. 'Now I know what it must feel like to be raped,' he told Prudence.

Among the letters of condolence he received he was astonished to find one from Professor Pfister, whom he regarded as the source of all his misfortunes. ' "There were two friends; there are two passers-by," ' the Professor wrote, 'but I trust I may still call you my friend, in spite of your disappointment over the Botticelli fresco, a disappointment much keener to myself. Though I am sure you are sufficiently philosophical to bear the loss of your paintings I wish to express my sympathy. While there is life there is hope, and your pictures may return. Pray to St Anthony. None of us should be excessively attached to objects in this short life. Old age is coming swift to meet us, says the proverb, and we should keep in mind that a shroud has no pockets. Let us then forget and forgive past disagreements.

'In my recent researches I have gathered more material about the history of your palace and the gonfaloniers, priors, ambassadors, prelates, captains, and knights of the Golden Spur who inhabited it in the past. It has occurred to me that this would fill an intriguing volume. May I venture to count on your collaboration? I have no literary pretensions but the talented Miss Prudence Royle has promised to polish my manuscript before it is sent to the publisher and Dr Cipollini has already agreed to sponsor an Italian edition. By the way, he informs me that your *Last Supper* is almost certainly by the hand of Orcagna. I trust it is still in your possession. In anticipation of a favourable reply, Yours, etc., etc.'

Martin replied briefly with an Italian proverb: 'God keep me from my friends: from my enemies I will keep myself.'

Prudence Royle attempted in vain to reconcile them as the Castor and Pollux of her coterie. 'Pfister rhymes with blister,' Martin said. 'I'm all blistered — he has brought me bad luck. First the refectory, then the robbery. Enough is enough.'

'He's a sweetie when you get to know him. Yesterday he proposed to me in the English cemetery, quite a surprise. I had no idea he could be so emotional.'

'And did you accept?'

'I'm between two minds. He certainly has a way with him.'

'Marry him and we part company. I'm finished with the Professor.'

Prudence clasped Martin's hand with a plushy pressure: 'Of course I'd rather marry you!' Her face shone like a glazed pink paper lantern, her nose needed powder, her chin a Gillette. Martin was overwhelmed with sudden panic: he tried to laugh it off. 'Don't be silly. We are both born bachelors. Can you see yourself as Mrs Pfister?'

'No, but I *can* see myself as Mrs Wilmer.'

Martin grinned as he recalled Nietzsche's aphorism, once quoted by Pfister: 'Thou goest to women? Remember thy whip!' He visualized a scene of flagellation with Prudence as the victim. From that moment he was never seen at her Thursday At Homes.

A Morning at Upshott's

'See you at Upshott's around twelve-thirty, okay?'

'I'll try to be punctual but you know what the traffic is at that hour. Jams without sugar.'

'Darling, I adore you. I'll be thinking of you all morning.'

'And I thought of you all night. Bye-bye for now.'

Upshott's was, and is, the most intimate bookshop in the West End of London, a meeting place for friends and lovers who could play at hide and seek, if necessary, behind its bulging shelves and topheavy columns of books newly arrived from the publishers, between tables neatly arranged with the latest volumes selected by Derek Upshott as best suited to the tastes of his regular clients — tastes predominantly influenced by his own.

Though the bottom was said to have dropped out of the book market there was no evidence of this at Upshott's. In spite of soaring prices hardback books were sold here to the exclusion of paperbacks. The basement was reserved for first editions, association copies, and rare folios with precious bindings, a haven for the serious bibliophile, but any book from Upshott's, whatever the subject matter, enjoyed a certain *cachet,* for Derek was an assiduous student of the current reviews and his literary standards were high. If you could not decide what to buy for a fastidious aunt or for a long voyage, you could safely rely on Derek's recommendation. His psychological flair with customers enabled him to separate the wheat from the chaff.

Some of the ladies who consulted him this morning were the chaff, and he needed much patience to deal with them, especially those who treated his shop like a public library or who merely came to gossip. 'Oh, there is nothing I love more

143

than a bookshop,' said one, 'and yours has such atmosphere. At home I've no leisure for reading. But as soon as I go out I steer straight for your emporium: it's so restful. Here I can browse and dream and forget that I'm dreaming. You should christen your place *Escape*.'

'I wish you would escape elsewhere,' he was tempted to retort. Another complained about a recent purchase: 'I grant you it is well written, but it is full of impossible situations and I didn't like the ending. Do find me something cheerful for a change. One may read for self-knowledge and spiritual satisfaction but one also wants a spice of entertainment.' Turning towards a newcomer, she exclaimed: 'Hullo, Daphne, what brings you here so early? How well you are looking. I've always envied your peachbloom complexion.'

'Actually I've an awful hangover, but I'm glad it doesn't show. Being at a loose end I popped in for something to read. Apart from cookery books there's so little worth wasting time on. One is driven back to Jane Austen.'

'I've just been grumbling about the novel that won the Phoenix Prize. So depressing.'

'They're all depressing. I shall have to give up modern fiction, yet here I return, still hoping for a pleasant surprise. Derek is a terrible tempter, he leads one on. Who buys all those heavy coffee-table books I wonder? They are getting more and more sumptuous but where is one to put them? I've so little space in my flat . . .'

The telephone was ringing and while Derek went to answer it — ('No, I'm afraid it is already out of print but a second impression is due. If you insist on a first edition I'll have to advertise') — Heather Carruthers, his winsome secretary (but not, as some suspected, his mistress) was addressing a batch of labels in the back room, which was even more cluttered than the front room. A jaunty little man in a grey bowler hat stumbled over the step and sent a pile of botanical books crashing to the floor. Without apologising, he said to Heather: 'Were those put aside for me? I'll buy them anyhow so don't

144

start blubbing. I need a drink. Have you got my poison in your secret cupboard?'

Derek peered round the corner with a broad political grin. 'Just up from Somerset? I hope you have come to stay. We have sold at least five hundred copies of your *Sun-dial* in the last few days. It's already out of print but I've hoarded a couple for your signature, if you don't mind.'

'Good egg. Won't you sign them for me? Your signature is as good as mine and far more legible. London makes me thirsty and I need a drink. Been on the waggon and it doesn't agree with my temper. Heather, dear, do pour me a pick-me-up.'

Christopher Blow claimed the privilege of a successful author who was also a generous client, vested in a furtive bottle of whisky. Miss Carruthers filled a tumbler for him. 'That's the right mixture. Here's to Upshott's! God bless. I say, Heather, have you been writing all these labels? What a morning's work. Derek's a tough taskmaster. And I've done nothing but bicker with my bank manager. Overdrawn as usual, I live on overdrafts. You see why I need a drink. Bung ho, little lady! Cheers!'

Christopher always managed to make a noise wherever he happened to be. His stentorian voice grew louder when the telephone rang again. 'Poor old Derek, need you answer? I never do.'

'Don't forget I'm a struggle-for-lifer,' said Derek. 'Half my stock is sold through the blower, pardon the pun!'

'Sounds like a party going on,' said a lady to Derek's bearded assistant Mike Robbins.

'It's only Christopher Blow,' he explained.

'I'd love to meet him. Do you think I could ask him to autograph one of his books?' Timidly she approached Heather's chair, which the novelist had occupied. 'I'm one of your most faithful fans. I've read all your books, some of them twice. My name is Griselda Lady Motley, of Motley Hall.'

Christopher blinked at her. 'Haven't we met before? I can't think where but your face is familiar.' He staggered to his feet

145

and lurched towards her with his glass of whisky. 'Want a sip? The other pubs aren't open yet. This is my private pub when I come to town.'

'No, thank you, but I've a little favour to ask. Would you sweetly autograph my copy of *Sun-dial?* It has meant so much to me, far more than I can express.'

'As a rule I refuse, but your name is so irresistible that I'll gladly inscribe it for you. My next heroine shall be called Griselda in your honour. Give me a pen — I mean a proper one — not a ball-point, all point and no balls.'

Derek appealed to his assistant, who appealed to various customers in the front room. In vain: they all had ball-points. Christopher shrugged his shoulders and wailed: 'Where have all the pens gone, with nibs like the good old J?', moaning in mock despair.

At last Mike Robbins came forward with an antiquated fountain-pen. Christopher scribbled with it all over Heather's labels. 'Ha, this will do, a vintage Waterman. Where did you find it, Mr Robbins?'

'I borrowed it from Mrs NcNab, our charlady.'

'Would she sell it to me? I'd like to keep it.'

'I'll have to ask her. She's making tea downstairs.'

When Mrs McNab appeared with a tea-tray, Christopher told her: 'I've taken a great fancy to your pen. May I buy it off you? I'll offer you twenty quid.'

'Sorry, sir, I wouldn't part with it for double that amount. It was found on my husband's dead body in Flanders during the First World War. He wrote all his letters with it, such lovely letters they were, all crosses for kisses. I lost them together with his photos in the blitz. Now I only have his pen.'

'I bet you don't use it. I'm a creditable author — isn't that so, Derek? — but I can only write longhand and I'm paralysed by a writing machine. Consider all the splendid books I could write with your venerable Waterman. Be practical, Mrs McNab, and sell it to me. Shall we say twenty-five quid?'

'Sorry, sir, it's my only relic of poor Mr McNab. He'd turn in his grave if I sold it.'

146

'Sheer sentimentality. Your husband would be proud to know it was in the hands of a famous author.'

'A writer ought to understand my feelings. I'm sure Dickens would.'

'I don't care a hoot for Dickens. Are we to embark on a literary discussion? Look what you've let me in for, Lady Motley!'

He inscribed the book with a flourish and returned the pen sulkily to its owner.

'Dear me, I've made a bloomer,' cried Lady Motley. 'I've got hold of the wrong book. This is by Iris Murdoch.'

'I'm afraid it will have to suffice. You can tear out the page and paste it in one of my own. Now I've a train to catch. Good-bye, everybody. Heather, give us a parting kiss!'

Lady Motley was mortified. 'He looked so nice in his photographs. I'm disillusioned,' she told Derek. 'But this has taught me a lesson. One should not meet one's favourite author. I'll keep the Murdoch novel as a curiosity, please put it down to my account, Mr Upshott. And tell me what's written in it, I've mislaid my glasses.'

' "For Darling Griselda, with undying love from Iris." '

'The little rotter! That's finished him for me.'

While she was denouncing him he rushed past her like a whirlwind. 'Help!' he cried. 'The Mogul's at the door. Hide me in the loo. I haven't the strength to face him.'

Cecil Cuthbertson, nicknamed The Mogul, had been at school with Christopher but they were not on speaking terms for the time being. Christopher had caricatured him as editor of *Transfusion,* the defunct organ of the avant-garde, and Cecil had parodied Christopher in *Damocles,* his anthology of aphorisms and obiter dicta. At school his flamboyant bosom had caused merriment at the swimming pool but this had since sunk to his paunch, for he was a notorious glutton. He had the rubbery face of a sea anemone, which was evidently an attraction to women: he could boast of three wives and several concubines, hence his nickname. He also had an impressive

147

following of aspiring authors who hung on his weekly pronouncements in the *Sunday Monitor*. Derek Upshott regarded him as his most reliable tipster for his verdicts were quoted as oracles by his clients. Consequently he welcomed his incursions with review copies from the *Sunday Monitor* for sale.

This morning he brought a round dozen selected for their high cost rather than for subject matter, books on birds and botany for which there was an increasing demand. Derek examined them carefully for the Mogul was apt to stain anything he touched with black fingerprints, coffee or tea. 'Fifty quid for the lot,' he said airily. 'A jolly good bargain but I'm short of cash. Here's one on *Graffiti* which should excite you, a phallus on every other page.'

'It's not in our line,' said Derek, glancing nervously at an old lady who collected Kate Greenaway. 'It can hardly be classed as literature.'

'But it throws light on the underworld of the human imagination. It is for the student of anthropology, a social document.'

'I call it anti-social. Please take it away. I shouldn't want my customers to see it.'

The Mogul guffawed. 'I'll save it for my girl-friends. But you'll keep the books on botany and birds? The country must be crammed with bird-watchers though I have never met one. Have you?'

'I meet plenty of queer birds in this shop,' said Derek. 'Some of them have to be watched.'

While Derek was writing a cheque for the Mogul a buxom woman in magenta trousers and a turban to match strode up to his desk.

'Shame on you,' she shrilled. 'Every other bookshop in London has my *Charlotte Corday* in the window. In yours it is conspicuous by its absence. Why am I being boycotted? You've been coining money from my best-sellers and I thought we were fast friends. What have I done to deserve such shabby treatment?' Her face was scarlet with fury. 'Ah, here is the nigger in the woodpile, Cecil Cuthbertson! You have behaved like a twerp: your review of my *Charlotte Corday* is outrageous. Fortunately you're not the only reviewer in Great Britain. You're just the mouthpiece of a decadent clique, eaten up with envy of creative writers like me. You're sterile to the backbone. Your *Damocles* proves it, a bundle of quotations strung together with platitudes. I despise you from the bottom of my heart.'

'Hell hath no fury,' Cuthbertson drawled. 'I seem to have hit the target.'

'I'll never speak to either of you again,' she hissed as she swept out into the street.

'A good riddance,' Derek muttered. 'That harpy has plagued me for years. I'm sorry to have missed the review in question: what upset her?'

'I called her the Marie Corelli of biographers.'

'You've a genius for the *mot juste.*'

'That diatribe was almost worthy of *The Sorrows of Satan.*' He looked at his watch. 'Angelica's late. She's driving me to Pilbury Towers for the week-end. Have you seen the place? *Ça vaut le détour,* as Michelin would say. Pure Victorian Gothic in a Repton park where exotic animals roam. The cellar is superb, the cooking fabulous, white truffles fresh from Alba, for instance . . .'

Derek thought gloomily of his sausage roll in the pub round the corner but considering the Mogul's paunch he did not repine. His own habits were abstemious.

There were at least twenty people in the shop this morning, stooping over the tables, craning their necks at the shelves, exchanging gossip or clamouring for attention. Outside the weather was bright and sunny: spring, the sweet spring, had already come to London. But Derek arrived by underground and went home by underground: he only saw the sun through the shop window. No Rolls Royce to drive him to Pilbury Towers! He doubted, however, if he would really enjoy such an experience. The Pilburys were fox-hunting folk and Cuthbertson merely cultivated them for their flesh-pots: he filled the role of family buffoon. When Derek left London it was for Provence — he would have to wait till summer. At a *mas* near Arles he would sunbathe and dawdle through the day, while his wife stood at her easel trying to paint like Van Gogh, the same cornfields swaying under a green sky to a chorus of cicadas. He sighed as he counted the months ahead. In Provence he hoarded enough sunshine to warm him through the London winter. The prospect cheered him in moments of dejection, yet he could not help being attached to the shop. When he sat over his accounts or tidied his desk after the day's work he was comforted by the presence of the books he sold for a living, and he was more often amused than bored by his customers.

Derek had imagined the hostess of Pilbury Towers as slender, tall and blonde, instead of which she was short and stocky with a strong square jaw and a muscular handshake. The Mogul introduced her and she explained that she was late because she had been shopping at Harrods — smoked salmon for the week-end. 'What a cosy little place you have here. That reminds me, Fritz Weinberg was raving about a sensational new biography of Charlotte Corday — he has bought the film rights. Have you got it?'

The Mogul and Derek burst out laughing. 'You've just missed the authoress. Cecil slated her book in the *Sunday Monitor* and she went for him tooth and nail.'

'Poor lady. Cecil is such a dreadful highbrow. I love him but I pay no attention to his reviews and I can't read the books he gives me. Proust is double Dutch to me, so is James Joyce. If you haven't *Charlotte Corday,* could you find me a good thriller. Where are your paperbacks?'

Derek looked at her sadly. 'Have you ever tried Wilkie Collins?' he suggested. *'The Moonstone, The Woman in White?* I only have them in first editions, more expensive than paperbacks.'

'Never mind, I'll take them though they look rather old hat. I can palm them off on Cecil if they're not my cup of tea.'

'I'm sure you'll enjoy them,' the Mogul assured her.

'That's what you said about Proust. Of all the long-winded bores he takes the cake.'

'Don't embarrass me, Angelica. I'll lose my reputation as a critic. Oughtn't we to be starting for the Towers? I should hate to arrive after lunch. What's on the menu? Books always give me an appetite.'

'Avocado mousse, duck à l'orange . . .'

'You make my mouth water, darling . . .'

So, talking of gastronomy, they departed hand in hand.

Simultaneously Christopher Blow left his prison in the loo. 'That was a long session,' he remarked with a hiccup. 'I finished all the whisky: now I'm plastered. Good night, sweet ladies, good night. Tootle-oo, patient Griselda.'

Having spied the volume of *Graffiti*, Lady Motley was still poring over its pages with popping eyes. 'I suppose you must cater to all sorts of tastes,' she told Derek, 'but I draw the line at this.'

'So do I. It was left on approval by an eccentric customer. I begged him to remove it and I regret that he failed to do so. As you see, we have been very busy this morning. I cannot keep an eye on everything. Please accept my sincere apology.'

More customers sauntered in with requests for *The Sun-dial*, and it was maddening to have to repeat that it was out of print. Not for the first time he cursed the improvidence of publishers.

As the morning wore on Derek's eyes looked older than the rest of his face and it was harder for him to control his annoyance with the potterers who picked up books, disarranged the shelves, and bought nothing. Lady Motley was the worst offender, and his patience with her began to ebb. Inquiries for Redouté's *Roses* and other rarities were dealt with by Mike Robbins, whose manner with tiresome customers was less urbane than Derek's. When a Hari Krishna gang trooped in with tinkling cymbals he threatened them with the police and chased them out. Since Christopher Blow had scribbled over her labels Heather had to address new ones while her boyfriend was fidgeting to take her out to lunch.

151

By twelve-thirty the front room was so crowded that the young couple who had agreed to meet there took refuge in the basement, which happened to be empty of bibliophiles at that time. Immediately they fell into each other's arms and embraced with all the ardour of pent-up frustration. The book-lined walls seemed a solid protection against the outside world. Quivering with rapture, the young man thought; what poet had written: 'The flesh is sad, alas, and I've read all the books'? He was hopelessly wrong: the flesh was jubilant, radiant, glowing with confidence. What were books to this vital force being fused into each other? The couple drank each other's spirit through the lips, she soft and yielding, he firm and masterful. They seemed to fill the sombre room with brightness. Oblivious of their surroundings they clung together billing and cooing till a loud nasal voice disturbed them. 'Hey, what's going on down there? Is that where you keep the erotica?'

'We don't go in for that sort of thing.'

'I heard funny sounds . . .'

The owner of the voice peered in. 'A nice little nook for necking,' he observed. 'That's the real stuff, much better than erotica. Carry on, folks. We only live once. Don't let me disturb you.'

Derek had already gone off for his sausage roll, leaving Mike Robbins in charge of the establishment. After refuelling himself with vegetarian sandwiches, vitamin pills, and cocoa, Mike took advantage of this calm hiatus to return to his hobby, the bibliography of a centenarian writer who existed solely in his imagination. This writer, for whom he had not yet invented a suitable name, was immensely prolific. Each of his productions was described, with a précis of its contents in elaborate detail. The extraordinary range of subject matter, from long epics to short pasquinades, allowed Mike to add a fresh item to his catalogue almost daily. At present he was concerned with a treatise on lycanthropy since he had dreamt of werewolves three nights in succession. So vivid was his account of these human transformations that he fancied he saw a werewolf creeping towards him with a vicious grin.

It was only a new customer who asked him for a copy of *The Sun-dial*. 'So sorry,' Mike replied. 'We should put an out-of-print sign in the window.'

Mike's flow of literary inspiration was interrupted in vain. For once he agreed with Sartre's dictum: 'Hell is other people.' Werewolves were Heaven in comparison.

The Narcissus Elegy

'The foie-gras was the best I ever tasted out of Strasbourg.'

'Did you try the white truffle tartlets? I thought them even yummier.'

'Everything was perfect of its kind. I felt I was in the Dordogne.'

The guests hovered round the remaining slivers of smoked salmon while an attentive waiter replenished their tumblers.

As usual the party was in honour of Adrian who had recited the latest canto of his 'Modern Metamorphoses', but nobody knew what to say about that. Whether it was hermetic or esoteric they could not decide.

'It was all Double Dutch to me but I liked the sound of it,' said Rita Goad, making a clean sweep of the chicken sandwiches. 'Adrian has missed his vocation. He should have been an actor or a singer.'

'A voice like his can make anything melodious,' Ellen Sprague assented. 'A pity he took up writing. Such twaddle really. I can't see any future in it.'

'At least Chloe believes in his genius.'

As usual Adrian's performance was a tour-de-force. In the vast music room of the Villa Belcanto he stood on a raised platform beside a lectern and Chloe sat in the front row close beneath him with glowing eyes. There was always an overture of nervous coughing. One woman sounded as if she were about to choke: with a handkerchief pressed to her mouth she tottered over the toes of her neighbours towards the door. Chloe followed her to fetch a glass of water. During this interruption Adrian proposed that everybody sing a catch he had composed, beating time with an arum lily:

'Don't let us tread on the daisies,
The dainty demure little daisies.
Don't let us tread on the daisies,
For soon they'll be treading on us, us, us,
For soon they'll be treading on us.'

When Chloe escorted the crimson sufferer back to her seat she hushed the gossips. There was frantic applause when Adrian announced that by special request he would read his 'Elegy on Narcissus'. Echo was in love with Narcissus, he explained, and he asked the audience to echo the last line of each stanza: 'Woe for the flower of gold with ivory petals!'

Merely to watch him reciting was an aesthetic pleasure. He had a mouth that many longed to kiss. The words did not seem to matter. Indifferent to popular success, he wrote in a verbal trance as the spirit moved him. The patterns of images that trickled from his subconscious often took Adrian by surprise. A few had been published in little magazines and their interplay of the verbal and the visual had been admired by practitioners of experimental writing. Having graduated from Dadaism, he wished to capture the mechanical effects of modern industry in block letters with indentations and zigzag spaces on the printed page. His punctuation was original: in his love-lyrics to Chloe every word was followed by a comma to represent a kiss. But such subtleties were lost in recitation. After his 'Narcissus Elegy' he recited a political poem: 'The sap has spread from our mangled map into the roots and branches of Ygdrasil. Rot the raw bourgeois huddled in their Hiltons!'

'Come to think of it, aren't we all bourgeois, Adrian included?' Rita Goad objected. 'Considering Chloe's fortune from sheep dip it seems ungracious . . .'

'It's just the trend of the times. He wants to keep up to date.'

'Radical chic, I suppose.'

Having spent their honeymoon in Florence, which Adrian voted 'the least bourgeois of cities', Chloe had bought him a spacious villa below Fiesole as a wedding present. 'I feel we were here in a former incarnation,' he said, 'don't you?'

'Dearest, this incarnation is good enough for me.'

The whole villa revolved round Adrian. Its every detail was devised for his mental and physical comfort. If he stretched his arms from his lofty studio, he could embrace the whole of Florence at a glance. Daily he revelled in this view of views, a monarch of all he surveyed. The villa's previous occupants had been British: the plumbing and electricity within, the close-cropped lawns and herbaceous borders without, were practical relics of their tenancy. Here he spent his mornings composing, and Chloe saw that he was seldom interrupted. When the Muse failed to come at his bidding he strolled up and down his open loggia in quest of the fugitive line, the essential word. That he published little and then privately, at Chloe's expense, seemed a proof of his superior quality. Chloe bound his manuscripts in vellum and as the years passed her enthusiasm for them never abated. She organized public readings and sold records of them for charity. The friends who were bewildered by this cult never dared to admit it. They nicknamed Adrian 'the Troubadour' because he looked romantic.

While Adrian tackled his "Modern Metamorphoses" the children, two girls and a boy, were kept out of sight and hearing.

'Hush, dears, your daddy's composing. Run out into the garden, Ronnie.'

'What is he composing, Mummy?'

'A masterpiece with a difficult name. One day you'll be very proud of it.'

'Nanny said one day I'd be proud of my tom tiddler. What did she mean?'

'You'll find out when you grow up, darling.'

Chloe could not help laughing. She must tell Nanny to be more discreet. Ronnie was too precocious anyhow, a diminutive edition of his father. The girls made more noise with their giggling and slamming of doors. The house was serenely quiet as soon as they ran out of it.

Again Chloe thought, how wonderful to be married to a genius! To her Adrian was all the poets she had admired at school rolled into one, Shelley and Byron and Keats, with the difference that he was absolutely modern. But hadn't they been modern in their time? When he read his poems aloud she was flooded in sweetness, but when she read them alone she was mystified. Though his handwriting was hard to decipher she insisted on typing everything he wrote: no secretary should come between them. While she typed the words sang and danced and swam towards her: in contact with his hieroglyphics she had a glowing sense of physical communion; she felt that she understood them with her instincts; everything became intensified, syllables were heartbeats. She was proud of acting as his literary agent, for in secret she negotiated with publishers to produce them in limited editions at her own expense. Needless to say they were soon sold out, since she bought up most of the copies for distribution among her friends. Being a beautiful heiress from Australia with a European education, she had collected friends everywhere. Her marriage to an obscure scribbler had disappointed them but they were very loyal.

Adrian was modest about his apparent success. 'All my stuff is out of print. Only Chloe knows how to wangle a copy out of the booksellers. I gather that my books have become collectors' items.'

There seemed no end to his 'Modern Metamorphoses'. In their Florentine bindings, they harmonized with the bibelots on drawing-room tables. Visitors picked them up, examined the fly-leaf and the dedication, and dropped them with a cynical shrug. 'Old Ovid's so much easier to read,' remarked Dr Finsworth. 'His stories are a bit far-fetched and some are decidedly off-colour, but he was a poet's poet. Will the same be said of Adrian? I doubt it.'

'Such a shame that Ovid was sent into exile,' said Ellen Sprague. 'Dante too, though the Florentines never stop quoting him.'

'All poets are exiles and Italy's still their paradise. Adrian belongs to their fraternity though I have yet to grasp what he is driving at. I suppose one should be a psychiatrist.'

'His *Narcissus Elegy* is obviously autobiographical. Adrian's madly in love with himself.'

'Surely he's in love with Chloe?'

'He sees his reflection in her doting eyes.'

'And in the adoring eyes of Monica, Jessica, and a bevy of younger girls. He's a shameless philanderer. I wonder Chloe's not jealous.'

'Why should she be? She holds the moneybags. Competition keeps her on the *qui vive*. Besides, he never goes too far with his fans.'

'I'm not so sure. I reckon that sofa in his study could tell a few tales.'

So they gossiped in the interval between one Canto and another.

'Hanged if I know why I attend these highbrow junketings.'

'I know why I do. Let me recommend the mint julep.'

'My missus drags me here. She's got a crush on Adrian.'

'You'd better watch out!'

At their co-educational day-school the children were teased about their father's poems. One boy purloined a copy of the 'Narcissus Elegy' from his mother and showed it to his classmates who found it exceedingly droll. Ronnie told Chloe about it and asked her: 'Why does Dad write such poppycock?'

Chloe looked very solemn. 'Never say that again. What he writes is too deep for you to understand. It is even too deep for me. But it's full of metaphysical meaning, in fact it is sublime. Tell your schoolmates that they are noodles.'

'What's metafuzzical, Ma?'

'Stop quibbling and take it from me that your father is a genius, a man in a million.'

Ronnie grinned incredulously. Why couldn't Daddy write something they could understand? They had urged him to write a detective story with flesh and blood characters but it

158

was a fiasco. The scene was laid in Sardinia with all the conventional trimmings, and the plot was contrived with mathematical precision, including two cases of mistaken identity, several murders, a violent kidnapping, and plenty of local colour. But his children, more familiar with crime fiction than Adrian, treated it as a joke and roared with laughter. So he returned to the world of mythological reverie in which he felt at home. But the abortive detective story had diverted his stream of imagery. He wrote a number of beginnings and tore them up.

Chloe peered through the window and noticed his air of dejection. 'You've been overworking, dear,' she called. 'Come out and smell the jasmine and relax.'

Overworked? He had only written a few lines. Yet he was aware of an unaccountable fatigue. That subconscious on which he relied had gone on strike. His eyes wandered to the shelf of his published works, all so slim, yet they gave him a sense of bloated satiety. Had he written himself out?

Chloe called from the garden again: 'I'm not interrupting, am I, darling? You should take a morning off once in a while. What a day for Siena or San Gimignano! Or we might lunch at Certaldo with the spirit of Boccaccio.'

'I'd rather stay here and lunch in the loggia. I'm ready for a very dry Martini.'

'I'll fetch Rita's cocktail shaker. By the way, Rita rang up.'

'What's her latest gambit?'

'She has an American professor in tow who's dying to meet you.'

'A mere pretext to waste my time. Let's forget it.'

'He has written a critical study of what he calls your "oover" and he wants your approval and permission to quote. I really think you ought to see him.'

'It's too soon. I haven't written my masterpiece yet.'

'Stephen Drystick — that's his name — considers you a contemporary classic and I promised Rita to arrange an interview. Don't disappoint me!'

'I'll bet he's a bore. All Rita's friends are bores.'

'It won't hurt you to meet him. Do it just to please me.'

Adrian kissed her in token of consent.

The learned young professor turned up that afternoon with a tape-recorder, a camera, and a bottle of Kentucky Bourbon. 'I can't tell you how much it means to me to meet the author of "Anamorphoses,"' he said. 'I reckon I'm the first academic in the States to recognize your genius.'

'I'm only a dilettante who writes for a few friends.'

'You must count me among them. I've blown my little trumpet in your honour, and my whole seminar at Hubbard hopes you will pay us a visit. We're a growing community of poetical research associates and your name is already inscribed on our roll of living celebrities.'

Adrian was disconcerted by the Professor's monologue. Moreover he was puzzled as to how the limited editions of his works had reached Hubbard College, Ohio, of which he had never heard. As Rita's interest in literature was confined to cookery books he could not imagine that she had been an intermediary. Actually she had bought his books for friendship's sake and sent them to her son at Hubbard College, who had given them to Stephen Drystick, his professor of literature. In his quest of the *dernier cri*, the professor was thrilled to the core. There and then he decided to boost Adrian as his personal discovery. He delivered a course of lectures on the subject in which Adrian was compared favourably not only with Ovid but also with Ezra Pound, and the professor's eloquence was very persuasive. Adrian's 'Narcissus Elegy' became particularly popular with both sexes of students.

News of this had reached Chloe, who had discussed its possible developments with Rita in private. Recently she had been worried by Adrian's dejection about his work. No contemporary review had ever mentioned his name; no anthology had included one of his poems. It was as if that series of slim volumes had never been heard of outside the small colony of Florentine expatriates. Though he was too proud to

160

complain, in his heart of hearts he had expected a modicum of recognition.

Now Hubbard College, Ohio, was blazing the trail for Oxford and Cambridge, since Professor Drystick had brought his typescript of 'A Study of Contemporary Genius' for Adrian's perusal.

'I'd be privileged if you would read it through and make suggestions before it goes to our college press. It has been a labour of love — I guess I have the pioneering spirit. I flew here especially to meet you but I'm afraid I have a tight schedule. Could you examine it inside a week? I dare not trust it to our erratic mails.'

Adrian glanced complacently through the contents. Elaborate footnotes doubled the length of every chapter and all his writings were listed with exact dates in the index. Young Drystick had done his home work thoroughly.

Chloe said: 'I'm Adrian's secretary as well as his wife. We'll enjoy reading it together.'

The professor thanked them effusively and proposed to toast the projected publication in an 'Old Fashioned'. But I've a supplementary favour to ask. 'Would you mind posing for a photograph?' The pose was repeated with variations till he ran out of film.

Adrian sat up all night reading the professor's exegesis of his life work. The more he read, the more he marvelled at his own achievement. Albeit inured to Chloe's raptures, he had not realized he was so important an innovator as Drystick set out to prove, quoting chapter and verse chronologically from his writings. Turning to the original sources he was filled with elation. He re-read his early Dadaist 'Cross-Currents' and agreed with the professor that it cast new light on his 'Collages' — the logical precursor of his 'Modern Metamorphoses'.

'Wonderful stuff, wonderful stuff!' he exclaimed, rubbing his hands with zest. 'I'm far more dynamic than I suspected. Dear Chloe was not mistaken.'

'At last you have found your ideal interpreter,' she said.

Both congratulated the professor and gave his book their *imprimatur,* to which Chloe furtively added a generous cheque.

Drystick had not only restored Adrian's flagging self-esteem, he acted as a stimulus to further creation. He began to write again as in his adolescence: the adrenalin flowed copiously from his subconscious and he looked younger than his age. It was Chloe who began to look older.

The final publication of Drystick's *opus* was celebrated with a grand display of fireworks on the terrace of Villa Belcanto, which the neighbours mistook for a religious festa, as in a sense it was. Again the lavish buffet was besieged: the foie-gras, the white truffle tartlets, the smoked salmon, were devoured with greater relish than Drystick's expensive tribute to the host, copies of which were on sale by the entrance. A case of Kentucky Bourbon from the faculty of Hubbard College was much appreciated by all, and the American contingent regaled the party with negro spirituals.

A Study of Contemporary Genius was reviewed at length in the *Times Literary Supplement,* and other journals followed suit. It was unusual for a British writer, of whom nothing was known in his native land, to be crowned as a laureate by an American academic, and the Oxbridge academics pricked up their ears. There was a sudden demand for Adrian's 'Metamorphoses' which no London bookseller was able to supply. He received flattering proposals from English and American publishers, and he was invited to give readings on both sides of the Atlantic. His last poem, an anamorphic version of Theseus and the Minotaur under the inspiration of Picasso, won the prestigious Higgins Poetry Prize, which ensured its selection by leading book clubs in the English-speaking world. Since the revised edition of Drystick's 'fundamental assessment' there were whispers of the Nobel Prize.

Whether it was due to his billowing acclaim or to the approach of middle age Adrian had grown physically stouter. He had a new trick of flashing his eyes like torches on interviewers, thrusting his shoulders back and crossing his arms. Chloe, on the other hand, had grown thinner. She had an enormous pile of Adrian's correspondence to deal with and though she refused to admit it she felt exhausted. This was apparent in her languid gait, her drooping mouth and eyelids. More frequently she had taken to resting at full length on a divan, completely motionless, with closed eyes.

So long accustomed to Chloe's ministrations, Adrian was vexed when she persuaded the plainest of her friends to step into the breach as part-time secretary. While Ellen Sprague could cope with his fan-mail she was incapable of deciphering his script, so Chloe had to dictate to her. An ardent feminist, Ellen was outraged by Adrian's masculine egotism. 'It's high time you called a doctor,' she told him. 'Can't you see that Chloe's worn out? She has never looked so poorly.'

Chloe would not hear of any doctor and Adrian resented the mere suggestion. Plain women were apt to be impertinent, he reflected.

'Change your oculist,' he said. 'My angel has always looked ethereal.'

'I've been a Red Cross nurse and I assure you that something's wrong. Where's a thermometer? She certainly has a temperature. Feel her pulse. Let me summon dear Dr Finsworth.'

But Chloe was adamant. 'What I need is a whiff of fresh air. This room is too stuffy.'

'Ellen Sprague would make any room stuffy,' thought Adrian.

As Chloe moved towards the garden she stumbled on the steps and lay there moaning. Adrian and Ellen rushed to her assistance and lifted her as gently as possible. Evidently the pain was excruciating for her face was distorted and bloodless. 'Too clumsy,' she gasped. 'I'm so angry with myself.'

An ambulance took her to the nearest clinic where she was given morphia as her hip was fractured. The surgeon professed modified satisfaction with the result of his operation, barring unforeseen complications. The patient had been very brave.

Friends arrived with flowers and fruit and chocolates but Chloe was reluctant to see them for more than a minute. Ellen insisted on staying with her under the mistaken impression that her society was therapeutic.

Adrian was too intent on the composition of his American lecture to notice her rapid deterioration. Her smile was a grimace, her voice was almost inaudible, and she clutched at the sheets with fingers like claws.

After a week the buxom sister who had been on night duty caught Adrian by the sleeve and asked him if he could spare a few minutes to talk privately with Professor Pacchioni the surgeon. Rising from a desk piled with X-ray negatives, Dr Pacchioni shook his hand with mournful gravity. He was smoking in nervous puffs and he offered Adrian a cigarette. The operation was inevitable, he explained, but he could not have foreseen a complication owing to deficiency of calcium. The Signora's bones were very brittle, in fact they were diseased, and she would always be lame if not bedridden. The chances of a complete recovery were nil unless Adrian, as a believer, risked taking her to Lourdes. Miracles inexplicable scientifically still occurred there. But she could not be moved yet, she was too weak. 'You knew of course that she has high blood pressure and a tired heart,' he added.

Adrian was shattered. Chloe had seemed so energetic, organizing every detail of life at the villa, telephoning, typing his manuscrips, engaging servants. She had driven the car and kept the accounts, determined to spare him what she called 'the chores'. All he had done was to write, sometimes half a page a day, and make himself agreeable to their guests.

'I'm so angry with myself,' Chloe repeated. 'I feel stupefied most of the time. You will have to fly to New York alone, and I was longing to share the success you deserve, to hear the applause.'

'I wouldn't dream of going without you. I'll wait.'

'But you *must* go. Promise!' She broke down and sobbed. 'Promise!'

164

'First you must get well.'

'I'll never get well if you cancel so vital an engagement. It is very peaceful here and the doctor said I needed a good rest. The sisters are angels. Let me sleep.'

Tears came to Adrian's eyes. He was exceedingly sorry for himself. Without Chloe at the villa he felt helpless and the servants took advantage of his plight. They were usually out when he rang for them; his meals were late and scrappy, yet the kitchen was full of the cook's family, eating and drinking and talking at the tops of their voices. The rooms had a forsaken air. Dust gathered on the furniture.

After his talk with the surgeon Adrian sent for his children in England, but Chloe died in the night before they arrived. One horrified peep into the mortuary chapel and Adrian fled. 'Chloe would not want me to see her in that condition,' he said to himself. Nor would he attend the cremation ceremony. The children witnessed it together and brought the ashes home in a silver urn. They dissuaded Adrian from burning his books and manuscripts, which might have been written by a stranger as far as he was concerned. Without Chloe's encouragement he never wrote another line.

His past life was safe in the hands of Professor Drystick. As for his future, he decided to grow a beard and become a philosopher. Patmos was his next destination.